JAKEDERIA FERRELL

Karmastically In Love

First published by Jakederia Ferrell 2022

This novel is entirely a work of fiction. The names, characters and incidents portrayed in it are the work of the author's imagination. Any resemblance to actual persons, living or dead, events or localities is entirely coincidental.

First edition

This book was professionally typeset on Reedsy.
Find out more at reedsy.com

Contents

One

Chapter 1

"Hey baby." Jakeshia said with a puzzled expression.

"What's up Jakeshia?" Raoul responded with an empty look.

"What you been up to this morning?" Jakeshia asked as she walked towards her man.

"Um… nothing, just been sleeping." Raoul said as he gave a phony yawn.

"Are you being dishonest?" Jakeshia picked up her purse and was ready to leave.

"Naw baby, I'm serious!" Raoul looked as if he was going to faint.

"Oh, you're telling the truth, are you? Okay. Why are your eyes bloodshot?" Jakeshia raised her voice, obviously upset.

"I…" Before Raoul could say anything, Jakeshia interrupted him.

"I know you weren't home last night. One, you look like you have a hangover; two, you don't have any liquor in the house, and three, I'M OUT!" Jakeshia stormed out of his apartment in a rage, but before she could get to her car, Amber stopped her.

"Hi Jakeshia, how are you?" Amber was Raoul's ex-girlfriend.

"How do I look, and how did I sound in Raoul's place?" Jakeshia didn't like Amber too much, but she was not the type to be disrespectful.

"Oh, I'm sorry. I thought I might be able to cheer you up." Amber was trying to put on her good voice.

"You, out of all the people, are going to cheer me up? Bitch please." Jakeshia hopped in her car and drove off. Little did Jakeshia know, Amber's best friend had just moved into Raoul's neighborhood.

Jakeshia arrived at her home in Lithonia, Georgia. She lived in a three story house with two roommates. Teresa and Mya had been her best friends since middle school. All three of them went to Spelman College in downtown Atlanta. Teresa was majoring in psychology, while Jakeshia and Mya were majoring in medicine. Jakeshia and Mya were both nineteen years old, and Teresa was twenty.

"Anybody home?" Jakeshia had calmed down since she left Raoul's.

"Who is it?" Mya and Teresa were at home.

"Who does it sound like?" Jakeshia smacked her lips as if she was mad.

"We got a surprise for you, girl!" They were whispering to someone in the background.

"Well, can it wait? Raoul and I just got into it." Jakeshia knew her friends were tired of her and Raoul's dysfunctional relationship.

"This might make you happy…very happy." The girls were coming down the steps slowly, smiling.

"Are you ready for your surprise to come down the steps!" Jamaal appeared at the top of the staircase.

"Hey Jamaal!" Jakeshia was excited; she hadn't seen him in seven months.

"What's up, baby girl?" Jamaal had had a slight change in his face structure.

"How was the war in Iraq?" Jakeshia was happy that Jamaal turned out okay.

"It was a struggle, but I made it through." he said and started to look sad and frustrated.

"There's something different about you…" Jakeshia was trying to put her finger on the distinctness in his face.

"Well, we were making an attack in Baghdad and….I got shot in the jaw. That's why I am back so early." They were all quiet.

"Well sweetie, we're just happy you're alright." Teresa was shocked at such sad news.

"A Mama's Prime Time is about to open up in an hour. Anybody up for some fun?" Jakeshia was a party girl and good at making people happy.

"I'm sorry Jakeshia, but I ain't up for it." Jamaal looked tired as he responded.

"Alright, I guess I'll see you later. I know my two girls are up for it." Jakeshia knew they were dying to go see Usher.

"Fa'sho girl, you know how Usher put it down." All three ladies gave Jamaal a hug and got dressed up.

"Ooh Jakeshia girl, it is freezing out here!" The ladies were standing in a line outside of Prime Time.

"We'll be in soon. I'm about to use my good looks to get us in quicker." Jakeshia was a dime and always used her good looks to get what she wanted.

"Hey you, you're clear to pass." a deep voice spoke to Jakeshia.

"My two friends clear to come in?" She was smiling as she walked out of the crowd.

"Um, they can if I get them digits." the mysteriously hypnotizing man replied.

"Sure, just don't call too late. I'm a college girl." She didn't want him to have her number, but this could get her and her friends in free every time they came.

"That's a bet, I'll give you a call tomorrow." The man was speaking as they walked inside the club.

"Ooh that's my song! Hey, get low, that's what I'm talking about." Jakeshia was a party girl and didn't care how she danced.

"What's up Jakeshia and friends." a ghetto and sexy voice came from behind them.

"Who...hey Marvin, what you doing here? Aren't you supposed to be somewhere trapping?" Marvin was the local trapper.

"Don't try me like that shawty." Ghetto as hell, but sexy for sure.

"Why you always telling someone to stop trying you? It's the truth, if I'm trying you then you trying yourself." Jakeshia was very intelligent and used her intelligence to win in all conversations.

"Man, shut up! You need to be a lawyer instead of trying to work with them snotty nose children." Jakeshia was pursuing a degree in pediatrics.

"Stop it, I love me some children." Children were always her main choice in life, but she wasn't ready to have her own.

"How about we have one of our own?" Marvin loved to flirt, especially with Jakeshia.

"In your dreams, lover boy!" Flirtatious, that she was, but she would never give Marvin a try.

"Anybody want me to buy them a drink?" While he was talking, the girls were headed to the bar.

"What you think?" Jakeshia caught an attitude but was only playing.

"Look here, Anna Mae, my foot going to be up your ass in a minute if you don't sing this song right." 'What's love got to do with it' was one of Jakeshia's favorite movies, and she was always intrigued when a person used one of the movie's phrases.

"I...I...I'm sorry Ike." Everybody burst out laughing.

"Man, what kind of drink do you want?" Marvin was so hypnotized by her looks that he forgot she was underage.

"I would like some Hypnotic mixed with Hennessy." She wasn't much of a drinker, but when she got her hands on some Hypnotic it was on and popping. Marvin told the ladies to go sit at a table so the bartender wouldn't ask for their ID. A few minutes later he arrived at the table with three Incredible Hulks, a mixture of Hypnotic and Hennessy. While Marvin was passing out the drinks, Usher appeared on the stage.

"Usher know he lookin good! When 'Yeah' come on I'm gone have to get on that stage." Jakeshia got up with her drink and walked to the stage.

"What's up ladies, I'm gonna need a couple of y'all to come on the stage with me." Usher was looking around to see who he was going to choose.

"I think you three ladies will be just perfect." It appeared that Usher was pointing at Jakeshia and the girls.

Questioning his choices, Jakeshia asked, "Are you talking about us?" Seeing Usher's domineering smile, Jakeshia put down her drink and got her two friends to come on the stage.

"Hey Usher, how are you, handsome?"

"I'm much better now that you're in my presence." Usher responded with a kiss on her right hand. "Alright everybody, y'all ready to have a good time?" The crowd was screaming while dancers got into place. As the music started playing, Jakeshia was shaking like she never had before. Usher came behind her and started to dance with her. She got even wilder so she could show him what she was working with. Based on his expression, Usher was feeling every move. "Ohhh, that's what I'm talking about, I need her on my squad." Usher talked about Jakeshia as she put on a show of her own. "What's your name Miss?" Usher gave her a handshake and kissed on the cheek.

"Jakeshia Carter!" Her baby voice was coming out as she smiled.

"Y'all give a round of applause for Jakeshia! She did a phenomenal job along with these other beautiful queens on the stage." Usher had the biggest smile on his face as he gave the three ladies backstage passes.

"So, Jakeshia, what are your plans for the rest of this evening?" He was a smooth talking, sexy walking, debonair player!

"Shit, probably just hit a club or a bar."

While staring into his eyes, she winked. "Just wondering if you'd like to head to my crib with me real quick." He was so gorgeous while licking his lips with his shirt off. Jakeshia had the opportunity of hanging with one of the greatest R&B singers and performers, why would she ever turn this proposal down.

While grabbing her things, she asked, "What about my girls?" Teresa looked drunk and Mya was drunk.

"Don't worry about that girl, we can just take your car to the house." the half woke Teresa spoke for the two. Usher said his goodbyes as he gave Teresa and Mya a hug. Jakeshia gave her friends a hug as she and Usher left the building.

"Wow!" Jakeshia was amazed at the beautiful marble, crystal, and glass that was neatly placed on the ceiling and walls.

"Amazing, isn't it?" Usher pushed open a mirror that hanged on the wall, which was a hidden closet.

"What's that, some secret hiding place?" As Jakeshia walked into the room she was again astonished, but this time it was by the many pieces of jewelry and accessories for both men and women that were placed on shelves.

"You want to go with me to a business party?" Usher picked up a sequin dress and a blue and white mink, he smiled slyly while placing the mink on her arms.

"Um yeah, but I don't want to wear this woman's clothing." She took off the mink and gently placed it in his hand.

"This doesn't belong to anyone. I bought this stuff specifically for the winner of my dance contest…which is you." He slowly wrapped the mink back around her.

"Ohhh, so that's why you wanted to come back to your place." She peacefully moved towards him for a kiss.

"Hold up now, this ain't going to work." Usher put his finger on her lips to stop her. "Shit, I know, the liquor starting to kick in." They both started to laugh as she fell to the floor.

"Can I go take a cold shower real quick?" She was still laughing as she tried to stand up.

"Whatever you wish, pretty lady." The two slowly walked out of the closet, Usher helping Jakeshia every step of the way.

"Do you have any ginger ale for my stomach?" As they were headed past the kitchen, they noticed the chain was off the front door.

"Um, didn't I place the chain on the front door?" They looked suspiciously around the kitchen.

"Yes, you did. Was there anyone here when we arrived?" He put the chain back and walked upstairs to his room.

"What the hell are you doing here this late?" Jakeshia rushed upstairs to see what was going in.

"Don't be alarmed Jakeshia, it's just my brother. And I thought he was going to our mother's." His brother was about to respond before he saw the beautiful woman standing in the doorway.

"I am, and who is this stunning woman?"

Usher smacked his brother upside the head, "Don't worry about all of that, scrub." His brother fell off the bed and balled up his fist.

"I bet if I asked Chili from TLC, she'd agree you're the real scrub! And I'm telling Ma when I go over there." Usher took Jakeshia's arm as they walked to his room.

Once again Jakeshia was amazed by Usher's home. "Well dang, everywhere I've been in your house has had marble and crystal, this is so immaculate!" Usher handed her the dress along with a washcloth and towel. He gave her a peck on the cheek and told her that he'd be gone for twenty minutes to take his brother to their mom's house.

"Wow, you look stunning and sexy, I made the correct choice today!" Usher walked into the room as Jakeshia was putting on her jewelry.

"Why, thank you, and when are you getting ready?" He was looking through his closet which appeared to be 500 square feet.

"I will be ready in twenty minutes." He looked around the

room for his watch so he could check the time. He then went into the bathroom to take a quick shower and change his clothes.

"What time does the party start?" Jakeshia was ready to go turn up some more.

"Whenever you want it to." He walked up to her, took her into his arms, and caressed her body.

"Ooh, so it's like that?" They started to kiss as he picked her up to take her to the bed. He laid her down as he went into his nightstand to grab a condom. After putting on the condom, he kissed her gently while sliding inside of her. Jakeshia moaned, but just then felt a vibration on her hip. Soon enough, she woke up from her dream. *Damn*, she thought.

"Hello, can I speak to Jakeshia?" She looked at the number as she wiped the drool off the side of her mouth. After clearing her eyes, she looked to her side and was surprised to see Usher driving. It felt so real, like she really thought she was about to get it on with Usher baby.

"Who is this?" she asked, confused about receiving a phone call so late.

"This is Jamison, the dude you met at Prime Time." She instantly became irritated.

"Didn't I tell you not to call me late! I have school tomorrow," she smacked her lips in disgust.

"My bad boo, I just wanted to speak to you so bad it slipped my mind. I'll call you back tomorrow beautiful, you have a goodnight." He sounded sad, but she really didn't care how he felt. Jakeshia had had enough disrespect from dudes to last a lifetime.

"Alright, bye!" She hung up the phone in relief.

"How long was I out?" Jakeshia didn't remember anything

after putting on the dress Usher gave her.

"About forty-five minutes." They arrived at a gate with the letters JT on it in gold. Jakeshia immediately got excited and nervous at the same time. She couldn't imagine meeting Usher and Justin Timberlake in the same night. Usher showed his license to the two men standing at the gate so they could gain access. As they entered and drove up the winding driveway, Jakeshia couldn't help but stare at the luxurious cars parked.

They arrived at a stunning mansion with all stone siding. The home was filled with life, laughter, and a wide spread of hors d'oeuvres. All attending guests were dressed to impress with glistening wrist and ears. "This is nice, do you always go to parties like this?" Jakeshia was in total awe about every detail down to the red carpet that trailed outside. "When I have time, I try to attend these events, but it's difficult with my busy schedule." Usher's Confessions album went diamond in the U.S. and received several accolades in other countries. He was so dreamy and such a hard-working man.

They left the party around 4 a.m., and Jakeshia had such a great time that she forgot about her midterms. She had to be up in three hours in order to get to school on time. "Tonight, was simply amazing! From your performance at Prime Time, the way you've treated me, and now this party!" Jakeshia was on cloud nine and did not want the fun to end.

"I'm glad I was able to please you. You're a beautiful lady and such a kind soul." Usher rubbed his eyes in exhaustion.

"I really want to thank you for this wonderful experience, but it is time for me to turn in. I have my midterms tomorrow, and I'm determined to ace them." Jakeshia put her address into the GPS so Usher could be guided to her house. As they drove away from the extravagant home, she began to doze off.

Chapter 1

They arrived at her house around 4:45 a.m. Usher shook her shoulder gently and called her name. Jakeshia woke up feeling like she was in the twilight zone. Her night was surreal, but she knew she deserved the enjoyment it brought. She said her goodbyes to Usher and thanked him again for being such a gentleman. By 4:56 a.m., she was undressed and in her California king.

Two

Chapter 2

Jakeshia made it to school by 8 a.m. to enter her class before the doors were shut. She had a massive headache from a lack of sleep, but that wasn't an excuse to miss her midterm that was worth fifteen percent of her grade in biology. She quickly grabbed a copy of the exam, took out a pencil, and got to work. After an hour and a half, she completed the 200-question midterm. Jakeshia left the room feeling confident and headed to the student center to take a power nap before her next class.

Shortly after arriving at the center, she discovered that a nap was not in her plans. There was a rally going on about financial aid. Hundreds of students gathered to devise a plan for receiving more grants and scholarships, since the amount rewarded had decreased recently. Fortunately for Jakeshia, she was still able to receive her full ride scholarship for academics. She had graduated high school with a 3.9 GPA and was seventh in her class. As long as she maintained a 3.0 GPA in college, she had no worries.

While walking past the stage she bumped into a buff, hand-some guy. Although Spelman was an all-female school, many guys from Morehouse and the surrounding colleges loved visiting the campus.

"My apologies, Miss…" The gentleman reached his hand out for a handshake and hinted at getting Jakeshia's name. She hesitated at first, then proceeded to shake his hand and give him her name. "That's a beautiful name. I'm Michael. It's my pleasure to meet you." He had a genuine smile with excitement in his eyes.

"Nice meeting you as well, Michael. What brings you to Spelman?" Jakeshia didn't usually entertain guys, but he was so polite.

"I heard there was a financial aid rally and thought I'd show my support. It's a shame how they had promised funds to so many people but changed their aid with little notice." *Damn*, was all she could think. This man came to an all-women's school to support a movement that he couldn't benefit from. She was impressed and shocked at the same time.

"So, what school do you attend Michael?" Jakeshia wanted to know more. "I am in my third year at Morehouse studying Engineering Science. What are you majoring in, gorgeous?" The way words floated from his mouth was so stimulating.

"I am in the Spelman and Emory nursing program. I plan on being a nurse practitioner." She looked at her phone to check the time, and noticed she had fifteen minutes before her next class.

"Am I holding you up from something? I'd really like to exchange numbers so we can continue this conversation." Michael looked hopeful.

"I have a class in fifteen minutes. I've thoroughly enjoyed this chat and would enjoy exchanging numbers." The two exchanged numbers and said their goodbyes. Jakeshia didn't know what it was about him that she liked so much, but he had her attention.

Jakeshia made it home around 5 p.m. and was totally exhausted. As she entered her home, she swore she'd never stay out until 4 a.m. on a school night ever again.

"Hey, is anyone home?" Jakeshia hadn't seen her girls since she left Prime Time the night before. There was so much she had to share with them about her night, and the gentleman she had met on campus.

"Keisha, giiirrrl! Where have you been?" Teresa ran down the stairs to greet Jakeshia at the door, hand on her hips and head tilted to the side.

"Usher took me to some grand extravaganza at Justin Timberlake's house last night. The party was so lit, and he had me looking like a star!" They slapped five in excitement as Jakeshia told Teresa about her night. Teresa was in complete awe at all the details being shared.

"I wish Mya and I could've gone with you boo, it sounds like you lived a fairy tale last night." Teresa was so happy for her friend. These ladies were riders for each other and always wanted the best for one another.

"I wish y'all could've come too. I know we will get lucky again. Did y'all come straight home after y'all left Prime Time?" Jakeshia grabbed some water and took a seat in the den.

"Yes ma'am, we had to. I don't know how you stayed out all night when we have midterms this week. We got home around one, and I still woke up tired! I think those incredible hulks did the job for me sis." The girls loved to party, but they usually saved the fun for the weekend. A few minutes later, Mya walked in the house with a hand full of groceries.

"Hey ladies! I'm so glad this day is winding down." Mya had been complaining about studying all week. Unlike Jakeshia, Mya had to study extremely hard to retain a lot of the content for her classes. The two tried to enroll in the same courses since they were both taking a nursing path, but they didn't get any of the same teachers.

"Girl you just missed my story about last night. Let me fill you in." Jakeshia told Mya about the remainder of her night, then proceeded to tell the ladies about her introduction to Michael. Mya and Teresa were in total awe at how appealing Michael sounded. Although it wasn't a priority for any of the girls to get involved in any serious relationships, coming across a man with great manners in Atlanta was like seeing a unicorn. Atlanta was full of men and women who wanted to play a game. The men wanted to engage in sexual encounters with multiple women, and the women wanted to finesse the men out of a check. This was a rare city to find true love; not to mention, the HIV/AIDS and STD rates were extremely high! There's no way these ladies were tainting their vaginas by messing with some low down, local joker.

The girls sat and talked for another hour, laughing about things that happened in the past. "Do y'all remember that time I got carried out of Secrets and my wig fell off? We woke up the next morning at some random apartment and didn't know where we were!" Jakeshia could not believe she'd ever allowed herself to get drunk to the point she couldn't walk out of a club on her own. She was lucky that people didn't find it hilarious to record others' drunkenness back then. If she'd gotten that drunk now, there would be a viral video on WorldStar Hip

Hop. Before they knew it time had slipped away, and it was approaching 9 p.m. The ladies said goodnight and went their separate ways.

Jakeshia took a steaming hot shower and listened to some slow jams. While showering she broke down crying at how things in her life had transpired over the years. She was such an intelligent, strong, and ambitious woman. She rarely allowed her emotions to get the better of her, but she was so overwhelmed with sorrow and bliss. Growing up, Jakeshia lived with her mom Jacqueline, older sister Marissa, and older brother Raquan.

Marissa was seven years older than her with a different father while Raquan shared the same father as her. She also had four other siblings by her father Samuel. Her childhood was an emotional roller coaster. Although she was loved by her family, she never seemed to really fit in anywhere. Jacqueline worked long hours to provide for her three children, which caused Jakeshia and her siblings to miss a lot of bonding time. When Jacqueline did have time, she did make sure her kids participated in sports, enjoyed vacations out of state, and engaged in church activities.

Jacqueline was a go-getter and single parent for most of Jakeshia's childhood. Even till this day, Jacqueline worked fifty or more hours a week at her job. Although Samuel got all his kids together on weekends and school breaks, he too spent a lot of time away from his home. He found himself working long hours and after work the kids believed he went to go trick off on women. While Samuel was out living his life, the kids were taken care of by Tiffany, who was Samuel's girlfriend, or they were left to fend for themselves.

Jakeshia exited the shower, dried off, put on some coconut oil, and fell asleep. It was only 9:45 p.m., but she was emotionally drained at this point. As she drifted off, she had a nightmare about the time one of Raquan's friends tried to rape her.

It was a warm afternoon, and she remembered her friend Jasmine was over at her house while both their moms were at work. They were hanging out in the basement when Raquan and Manny came in to bother them. Raquan asked Jasmine to go with him to the laundry room and left Jakeshia alone with Manny. A few moments later, Manny got on top of her and attempted to take off her pants. She fought hard for what seemed to feel like forever, and she finally got him off of her. She raced off the sofa to open the laundry room door, and to her dismay Raquan was on top of Jasmine.

Totally confused at what she was experiencing, Jakeshia ran upstairs to lock herself in her room. She was only eight years old and did not know what had happened. She cried about Manny's actions and was upset that Raquan had obviously agreed to such a plan. What type of older brother would have sex with an eight-year-old while his friend was in another room trying to rape his sister?! Jakeshia couldn't remember seeing or speaking to Jasmine after that. She lodged the horrific memory in the back of her mind and never spoke of it to anyone.

If she had learned anything from that, she learned at a very young age that she couldn't trust her brother. She grew up to have a deeply rooted love/hate relationship with her brother that no one really knew about. Aside from this event, Raquan could be verbally and physically abusive towards his younger sister. One day, he was being annoyed by Jakeshia and decided to drag her across the floor by her braids, in front of his company. Another day, he bent and twisted her ankle so bad that it felt like it was going to break. After that incident, she called her dad to snitch, and of course the excuse "He was just playing" was given.

With a lack of male parenting, it was no wonder Raquan had multiple arrests and felony charges by the age of eighteen. He had gotten a minimal sentence for a statutory rape charge at fifteen, beat a murder case at sixteen, and only served five years for an armed bank robbery. No one knew what drove Raquan to commit these and other crimes. Jacqueline always made sure her kids did not go without. Through all that stress, the family always stood by his side with support. As Jakeshia got older and realized the damage that her brother caused, she was able to develop her own opinion, despite the love she had for him. She went from screaming "Free my brother" to "You get served what you deserve." Jakeshia always battled with her emotions because she remembered the good qualities about her brother, but she also could not respect his life choices. Raquan not only stole from strangers, but he even stole from Jakeshia and her mom.

Jakeshia suddenly woke from this nightmare crying with a dry mouth. She went downstairs to grab a glass of water to quench her thirst and sat at the kitchen table for a second. The clock on the stove read 3:08 a.m., which just so happened to be Raquan's birthday. She wondered if the universe was trying to send her a sign. She didn't speak to him often since he always came to her for handouts. She didn't understand how he had the nerve to ask her for money when she was a full-time nursing student and worked part time as a waitress at Arizona's. Her scholarships paid her way through college, but Arizona's made sure she could pay her part of the rent. Her mom had instilled hard work and ambition in her, and Jakeshia would never stop until she succeeded. People thought she was crazy and even boring sometimes because she focused so much on her studies. Jakeshia didn't pay them any mind though. While everyone clubbed and had babies, she was trying to get to some serious coin.

Jakeshia was back in bed by 3:30 a.m. and felt a lot more at ease. She dozed off and awoke in four hours to the sound of her alarm clock. She immediately went to the kitchen to start some old-fashioned oats on the stove, then went to brush her teeth and wash her face.

"Keshia!" Mya called out from the kitchen.

"I'm coming, my love." Jakeshia had just finished getting dressed and headed to the kitchen to finish off cooking her breakfast.

"Do you have any midterms today?" Mya inquired.

"Yes ma'am, I have my last two today." Jakeshia placed her oatmeal in a bowl with blueberries, cinnamon, and sliced strawberries. She wasn't a fan of sugar, so she liked to add fruit for sweetness and health benefits.

"Y'all have any midterms?" she asked Mya and Teresa, who were both munching on cereal.

"Girl yes, we both have our last three today." Teresa answered with frustration in her voice. "I'm so ready to get this testing over with. I haven't been able to sleep, and I need to pick up some extra shifts at work." Teresa worked as a sales associate at Forever 21. Though she didn't make much, she loved her discount.

Jakeshia finished with her midterms around 1 p.m. While she was walking to the bistro, she received a phone call from Michael. "Hello." She put on her baby voice to give off sex appeal.

"How are you doing queen? This is Michael." Man was his

voice enticing, and his vernacular spoke to her soul.

"I'm doing great! I finished my midterms today, and I know I aced all of them." Jakeshia felt very confident leaving her classrooms. She had studied and retained a lot of information from her professors' lectures.

"Wow love, that's great to hear. I'd love to take you to a celebratory lunch so we can get to know each other better." Michael sounded genuinely happy for her success. All Jakeshia could think about was how jealous Raoul used to get when she talked about school. See, Raoul never finished high school, but he did get his GED. He never thought school was for him but was very intelligent. Raoul preferred living the fast life selling street drugs and pharmaceuticals. Unfortunately, he never had the drive to invest his money into any legitimate businesses.

It was definitely time for Jakeshia to get over Raoul and build a future with a man who was willing to grow. "I'd actually like to do that. I could meet you as early as two-thirty. What restaurant did you have in mind?" Jakeshia loved to eat, but she would rarely take men up on their offers.

"Let's meet at The Sundial." Her heart skipped a beat. The Sundial was 723 feet in the air and rotated so you could get a 360-degree view of the city. She knew this restaurant was expensive and could not understand why Michael would want to take her there for lunch when they barely knew each other.

"What? The Sundial, Michael? That's a little over the top, don't you think?" Jakeshia really had to question this man. Raoul had money most of the time, but he never tried to take her out to fancy restaurants. His idea of a date was always Applebee's or Chili's.

"Sweetheart, there's no such thing as over the top when it comes to pleasing a beautiful, intelligent queen such as you."

There Michael went again with his play on words. It's like he knew all the right things to say, while using an inviting tone.

"Well thank you so much, I guess I will be meeting you at two-thirty at The Sundial."

Jakeshia arrived at Peachtree Street around 2:15 p.m. so she could be punctual. She had freshened up and changed her outfit on campus, so she didn't have to drive all the way back home. She always kept an overnight bag in her car in case of an emergency or a night out on the town. As she made her way to the lobby, she saw Amber, Raoul's ex, walking down the street. She couldn't help but think back to two years ago when she buried her younger cousin.

Jakeshia had been calling Raoul's phone to make sure he made it home safe, but he wasn't answering. Raoul had taken so many shots of alcohol to the head at the repast, and Jakeshia wanted to be sure that he made it home safe. She told herself that she'd just drive past his house to be sure that he was home safe. When she drove past, she was relieved to see his car, but Amber's car was outside too. Although she had recently broken up with Raoul, they were still dealing with each other and even claiming each other. She immediately parked her car and stormed towards his door.

Before she could bang on the door, she saw the silhouette of Amber and Raoul, and they were definitely having sex. She was so angry, heartbroken, and confused at what her eyes were seeing. How could he be sleeping with another woman? She twisted the doorknob, and to her surprise the door was unlocked. How fucking sloppy could this asshole be?

She walked up to his room and stood in the doorway, ready to rip both their heads off. After a good ten seconds, she finally spoke. "Hey you trifling, disgusting, disrespecting, classless motherfuckas!" She was in rage. They both stopped quickly and looked her way. Raoul didn't even have a condom on.

"Jakeshia, what the fuck are you doing here?" Raoul started to put his clothes on and walked her way.

"Nah, fuck all of that. What is this bitch doing here?" She pointed to the frightened Amber. Amber didn't want these types of problems. She knew Jakeshia could beat her ass if she wanted.

"Man, we don't even go together. You broke up with me remember?" Raoul was definitely single, but Jakeshia couldn't believe that he would be fucking someone else after they had just made love last week, and without a condom. All day long they had been consoling each other and wiping each other's tears. The disrespect and total disregard just made her feel like he never really gave a fuck about her.

"Yeah, you're right. Amber, just know, I'll be telling your girlfriend that your dirty pussy ass is over here fucking a nigga raw." Jakeshia left more peaceful than she arrived. She realized that she could not be mad at the situation, she just knew what type of energy to have with Raoul.

Jakeshia snapped back to reality as she entered the lobby of The Sundial. She smiled super hard because she was so grateful that she no longer dealt with Raoul's trifling ass. She was so ready to receive all the blessings that this next chapter in her life had to offer. She waited in the lobby for five minutes until Michael showed up.

"Hello beautiful, I'm so glad you came." Michael's hug was so loving and warm that Jakeshia almost melted.

"Thank you for inviting me, you really have me feeling special." Jakeshia blushed as they walked towards the hostess station. Michael told the hostess his name, and she walked them to their reserved table. The table had a spread of three different appetizers waiting for them under a food covering.

"Thank you." they both said to the hostess.

"Michael, this is really nice. You really put thought into this spontaneous lunch." She was in total awe at how detailed he could be for a last-minute meet up. He had a platter of oysters and crab cakes, wings, and a spinach dip.

"You're welcome queen, you really deserve this. It's very important that you nourish your body for sanity and to keep that intelligent brain of yours sharp." At that point Jakeshia was trying to figure out what planet Michael was from. What kind of man did these things and had such a way with words? Jakeshia excused herself so she could go to the restroom to wash her hands.

While in the restroom, in came no other than the scandalous Amber. "Hey, Jakeshia." Amber said excitingly. Now this bitch knew Jakeshia did not fuck with her. Jakeshia took her speaking as disrespect. How dare she continuously attempt conversations with someone she had wronged. For the life of her, Jakeshia could never understand how ignorant this girl could be.

"Girl, please don't speak to me as if we are friends. I don't like you. I never have, and we will never be anything." Jakeshia spoke as nicely as she could. She wanted to keep her composure so Michael wouldn't know anything about this encounter.

"Jakeshia, I'm sorry girl. I never knew that you and Raoul were dating any of those times." Amber sounded sincere, but so did every low life when they wanted you to believe them.

"Sweetheart, if that's the lie that helps you sleep at night, keep telling yourself that. But honestly today, and for the rest of my life, I will never give a damn about the things that you and Raoul did. I'm moving forward with my life and truthfully wish you the best. Good day love." Jakeshia dried her hands and left Amber looking stuck. Amber was one of those fake people who wanted everyone to like her. If you didn't like her, she would do and say conniving things to defame your character. One thing about Jakeshia was that you didn't want to fuck with her though. She would make you eat every bad thing you said. Anyone that ever wronged her always got a visit from karma.

"There you are, beautiful. I got worried for a second." Michael stood up to pull out Jakeshia's chair. He was the perfect gentleman.

"I'm sorry love, I ran into an old friend while in the restroom." Jakeshia wanted to move on with her date without involving Michael in any drama.

"Oh, that had to be nice. You should've invited her over for lunch." Michael was being too nice.

"She wasn't that type of old friend. Just someone I know but don't really get along with. But any who, let's dig into these wonderful appetizers. It's crazy that you ordered these four items, I love them all!" Jakeshia didn't want to sound too anxious, but the girl was about to smash.

"I'm happy to hear that queen, you deserve it all. It's a celebration." Michael raised his water glass for a toast.

"So tell me Michael, how did you become such a gentleman? I mean, it's not every day that a man your age knows how to treat a woman." Jakeshia took a sip of her water and patiently waited for his reply.

"Well, I truthfully believe that it's unfortunate that this has to be a question. The standard for men seems to be set so low that when a person of my caliber comes to the table, it's rare. I was raised in a household with my mom, younger sister, younger brother, and stepdad. I don't even address him as a stepdad or look at him any differently from my family. He rose to the occasion when my biological pops fell short. Being raised by my mom and dad showed me that a woman is to be respected, catered to, wined, dined, protected, and ultimately loved. Many dudes my age think that it's simpish to love one woman, while finding it cool to play a woman. The sad part is, we all came from a woman. I'd be a complete fool to ever want a man to mistreat my mom, sister, or grandmother. I worship the ground that my queens walk on. I always want to give light and love to everyone that I involve myself with and hope it's always reciprocated. I hope that answers your inquiry." Michael smiled as he gazed at Jakeshia.

"You gave me my answer and then some. It's very admirable that you have this perspective when it comes to women. My mom raised me and my two siblings with some help from my dad, but not as much as she needed. She still managed to make things happen. Would you believe me if I said my dad had approximately six kids?" Jakeshia laughed, because she knew Michael would be left confused with her question.

"What do you mean by approximately?" Michael asked, extremely perplexed.

"So I grew up with five of my dad's kids, one of them who is also my mom's son. The other four were by three other women. My dad has six confirmed kids, but word on the streets is that he has two younger kids that we have never met. Papa was a rolling stone, baby." Jakeshia burst out into song, singing the temptations 'Papa was a Rollin Stone.'

"Girl, you are silly. I feel you on that though. So how was life growing up with a crew living in different households?"

Michael seemed intrigued by Jakeshia's background. He was able to see his siblings daily and bond with them.

"It was pretty cool, I guess. We all got together at my dad's house many weekends and extended breaks. Although he wasn't there much, we would be with my grandmother, uncles, or stepmom. The funniest thing about my dad having all these kids was him having two sets of ghetto twins. I can tell by your face that you have no idea what a ghetto twin is. So, a ghetto twin is when you have a sibling who is the same age as you but does not share your birthday and most likely doesn't have the same mom." Michael looked even more confused after she dropped that bomb. "My oldest two brothers are three months apart, and I have a sister who is five months and five days younger than I am. They call it ghetto twins because it's ghetto and trash as hell to have kids the same age who are not biological twins."

Michael shook his head. "Okay, I understand. So it must have been pretty cool growing up with someone your age." Jakeshia shrugged her shoulders. "I don't think it made a difference. We weren't connected at the hip or best friends. We actually butted heads a lot as kids because she acted stingy. She was an only child in her household for eight years, so she was used to getting everything that she wanted from our dad and her mom. Plus, I don't think they disciplined her much."

The waitress came back over to take their food orders. "I'd like to order the Loch Dart Salmon." Jakeshia knew what she wanted without browsing the menu.

"I'll have the same." Michael hadn't looked at the menu either. The waitress walked away and the two began conversing.

"So, you like the salmon as well?" Jakeshia asked with a slight grin.

"I've actually never tried it, but I know a woman like you must have exquisite taste. I usually order the sea bass."

"You aren't lying about that. I can agree that I have great taste. Well, except when it comes to my choice in men." Jakeshia shook her head.

"Baby girl, your taste in men wasn't poor. God just gave you all the wrong men to prepare you to receive this strong man before you. If they hadn't failed you, we wouldn't be here today. I can't lie and act like I'm not happy that those dudes dropped the ball, because I'm here to pick it up, and I promise this will lead to a slam dunk." Jakeshia choked on her water. She had never experienced a man speak highly of himself in the regard of treating a woman like a queen. Michael talked a good game, but she had to tell herself to not get wrapped up in words. After all, every guy she'd ever dated filled her head with words that they never backed up. What made Michael any different?

"Thank you, Michael, I really appreciate all your kind words. I do want to say that I've heard similar things before. Just treat me right and be genuine, only time will tell where this friendship could lead us." The two ate their food and sat to talk for two more hours. They were all smiles and laughter. Jakeshia offered to pay for her bill, but Michael was a true gentleman and paid for everything. She had learned that it was okay to offer to pay your part of the bill occasionally, but the man's reaction to your gesture would let you know how chivalrous he was. When they finished up, Michael walked her to her car and said his goodbyes. He opened her car door, they hugged, he gave her a kiss on her hand, and he made Jakeshia promise to call him once she reached her next destination. Michael watched as she drove away.

Three

Chapter 3

Jakeshia arrived home shortly after six in the evening after she had sat in a little Atlanta traffic on highway I-20 East. She immediately went to take a shower after the productive day she had. She couldn't wait for her girls to get home so she could begin the conversation with that trick Amber but finish with her awesome date. She thought about Michael the entire ride home. Those butterflies he gave her were new and something she had never experienced. When she got out the shower, she moisturized with some Victoria's Secret lotion. She was feeling ultra-sexy and wanted to smell the exact same.

Jakeshia entered the kitchen to see Teresa playing some India Arie. "Yes, he is the truth, said he is so real." She started singing along to the soulful tunes. She absolutely loved India Arie. Her songs made Jakeshia feel like a woman, gave her the power to grow in love with herself, and helped her learn better qualities to look for in a man.

"Keeshia, hey girl!" Teresa squealed as she turned the stove top on.

"What it do, bay bay?!" They hugged and Jakeshia went to sit.

"So how was your day? Would you like some green tea?" The girls loved drinking green tea to aid in fat loss, lower the risk of cancer, and decrease the risk of heart disease.

"Girl, you know I could go for some green tea any day! Sis, I've had the most amazing day. So of course, you know midterms were today, and I just know I beasted on those. But when I finished my midterms, I received a call from Michael, you know the fine brother that attends Morehouse? Whew chile, he invited me out to lunch at The Sundial!" Jakeshia took a pause to allow Teresa to respond.

"Whheeeet?! So, the first time he took you out he chose The Sundial?! Okay bissshh, now where's the rest of this juicy tea?"

Teresa wasn't referring to any literal tea. "So, we met up at the The Sundial, and he had appetizers waiting on us at the table. When I say I felt so freaking special. Once we got situated, I headed to the restroom to wash my hands. Tell me why I bumped into that trick Amber in there. The bitch had the nerve to speak to me like we were cool or something." Teresa cocked her head to the side in disbelief at what Jakeshia just said. "I quickly told her about herself. Like girl, please don't act like you weren't helping Raoul's trifling ass cheat on me! After that I went back to the table to eat. Michael and I sat there for two hours getting to know each other. When I say the conversation with him just flows, and he's such a gentleman. I'm not used to people like him, he really has me questioning if he's genuine or not."

Jakeshia went to grab her favorite mug, which had 'sophisti-cated savage' written across it. She placed a tea bag in her mug, dropped a teaspoon of honey in, and poured in the hot water. She tried her best not to add unnecessary sugar to things and overtime learned to enjoy certain food and beverages for their own taste.

"I feel you girl. Dating in Atlanta is so scary. He does sound like a nice guy, so don't let your past experiences run you away from a possible good thing. I don't know any guy that would take you to The Sundial on the first date, and he didn't ask for any sex afterwards! Girl, you're winning!" They both burst out laughing.

"Girl, remember that guy I was talking to from McDaniel Street? No one would have ever thought we'd see him at lips as a damn drag queen! These men down here are undercover for no reason! I just don't understand why you lie about your sexuality in a city that's accepting and has so many options for the LGBTQ community. After I saw him there, I found out he was a slut with men and women. And to think, he was trying to have raw sex with me. Always wrap it up! Especially if you aren't exclusive, but I digress."

Teresa had been hurt her entire life. She grew up with eight siblings, a mom and dad who were both on drugs, and there was never any stability in her home. In her household she was the oldest but had three siblings that lived in other states. Teresa had to cook, clean, and watch her younger siblings every day. She honestly was a modern day Cinderella. Her parents verbally abused her, and her mom would occasionally hit her for no reason at all. Despite her childhood, she managed to beat the odds. Now here she was, a college girl estranged from her family. She felt bad for her siblings and wanted to continue to nurture them, but if she stayed around, she would continue to endure the abuse of her parents.

The girls sat in the kitchen and talked a while longer. Reminiscing about the past and how far their friendship had come. Jakeshia and Teresa met each other in the fifth grade, and they lived next door to each other until they graduated from high school. Before graduation, they had decided that they wanted to get a house together while they attended college. Jakeshia was always welcome at her mom's home, but she loved her independence.

"Teresa, I know I don't say it much, but I am so proud of how far you have come, girl. It's not every day that someone could grow up the way you did and overcome all of those obstacles." Jakeshia got up and gave her friend a hug.

"Aww, thank you baby. I promise I would not be where I am if it wasn't for having best friends like you and Mya. You two really keep me grounded and out of jail." Teresa used to fight a lot. She was from California and the gang banging in her neighborhood was crazy. Just imagine a nine-year-old getting cut on her arm all because she wore a specific color shirt. Although her parents were not the best, the one good thing they did was move to Lithonia, Georgia.

"That's what friends—I mean sisters—are for. Girl, I'm about to call it a night. I have to open at work tomorrow. If you see Mya's hot ass, tell her I said goodnight." They both laughed as Jakeshia went to her room and closed the door. She wanted to meditate for a few minutes before she went to sleep, so she turned on India Arie's 'I Am Light' and started doing breathing exercises. She was determined to stay positive, levelheaded, and focused.

The next morning, Jakeshia got up and headed to Arizona's dressed in all black. Since she was so responsible and efficient at most positions, her manager put her in charge on the regular. When she arrived at the restaurant, she had to prep different fruits and vegetables, roll silverware, and restock the bar. Her main position was a waitress, however the managers allowed her to fix alcoholic beverages. She was underage, but she knew how to mix a few drinks. The rest of the crew arrived, and Jakeshia designated sections to the servers. She always worked in the busiest sections since she could manage the crowd, plus it allowed her to make more money. Some of the female servers despised her because of her flexibility on the job, and of course many of the regulars requested her when they came in to eat or drink.

Jakeshia couldn't help it if she was a people person and knew how to run up her bag. She knew she had to pay her bills and spoil herself. She was grateful enough to get scholarships for school, but of course she had to maintain a 3.5 GPA or higher to get one-hundred percent of her schooling paid for.

"Hey Jakeshia, could I get booths two to ten today?" Melissa asked. Melissa had been working at Arizona's longer than Jakeshia, however she was not the best server.

"I'm sorry Melissa, the managers and I just don't feel like you are ready to handle that section, nor that many booths at one time." Jakeshia hated being the bad guy, but she was always willing to do whatever it took to advance at her job. The manager on duty arrived a few minutes later and called Jakeshia into the office.

"Hey Jakeshia, I really appreciate you for holding down the fort for us these past few months. John and I have decided that you are the perfect fit to be added to our managerial staff." Miranda smiled extra hard because she knew Jakeshia had not expected the news.

"Wow Miranda, I truly was not expecting to receive this type of news today." Jakeshia spoke excitedly but thought about all the responsibility that was required to be a manager. She wanted to continue to focus on school, so she did not know how her schedule would work out. "I am very thankful for this offer, but I will have to pass it up. With me being a full time student, there is no way I can manage to keep my grades up while being a manager here." Jakeshia looked sad that she couldn't accept the position. "Jakeshia, you are already doing so much for the company, we really should have given you this title. This new position will entail you doing everything that you currently do and working the same number of hours. The only difference will be your pay." Jakeshia jumped up with glee and hugged Miranda with gratitude. She was astonished that she would be making more money for the same amount of time and work. She worked her butt off at Arizona's but was not expecting that position.

After all, it was not a part of her endgame, just a job to get her through college. "I definitely accept the position. When can I start?" They both bust out laughing. Miranda printed off the job responsibilities and pay just to be formal, although Jakeshia went above and beyond the requirements. The ladies went their separate ways, and Jakeshia went to work, taking on her new position as a manager.

Jakeshia left work around 5 p.m. and immediately went to call Raoul. The phone rang twice before she hung up. "Dammit, I can't believe I just called this dumb ass dude's phone!" she yelled out loud to herself. She was so accustomed to telling all of her good news to Raoul, even though he didn't seem interested half the time. She had been dating Raoul when she first got the job at Arizona's. He would always ask her to bring home food from work, he especially loved their spinach dip. It was crazy how she would have to unlearn so many habits from the past three years of her life. Although three years was not a long time, it seemed like a lifetime since he was her first. Jakeshia wasn't saving herself for marriage, but everything seemed so right when she got with Raoul. And here she was looking like a complete fool for putting up with his inconsistency, cheating, and disrespect. As she pulled into her driveway, she promised she would never go through any bullshit like that again.

Four

Jamaal's Story

Jamaal was back at his mom's place in Lithonia when he woke up in a cold sweat. Fireworks had woken him up, making him think they were gunshots. He got out of the bed to go fix a glass of water in hopes that it would calm him down. Jamaal was severely suffering from post-traumatic stress disorder, also known as PTSD. During the war he had seen so many people get killed, critically injured, and families mourn. His accident only made his PTSD worse.

He got a glass of water and looked out of the living room window to stare at his neighbors who were randomly popping off fireworks. As he stared into outer space, his mind wandered off thinking about his tour in Iraq. When Jamaal arrived in Iraq, he had no idea what would be in store for him and his unit. They were told that they were going to protect the civilians and the United States from terrorist threats. About five days after they arrived, there was an order for them to take a convoy to attack a village eighty miles away from camp. Everyone was confused but they went to follow orders.

When they arrived outside the village, they saw armed men and children walking around. They surrounded the place from all angles and waited for the captain to give the order to attack. After sitting for two hours, they received the signal. The attack was started with fifteen hand grenades being thrown. It didn't matter if there were kids around, they followed the orders given.

Once the grenades went off, they stormed the place, shooting every armed person in sight. As Jamaal went through the village, he stopped in front of an injured little girl who looked about five years old. The girl was injured from the grenade explosions. Jamaal was frozen and in tears. She was in so much pain, so Jamaal picked her up and started to carry her back to their onsite doctor.

The captain saw Jamaal drop the girl off and immediately commanded him to go back to help finish the attack. Jamaal did not want to go back but did as he was told. This time in the village he was welcomed by a hail of bullets that he luckily dodged. As he ran for cover, one of the other soldiers was hit in the neck. Jamaal could not believe his eyes. He wanted to save his fellow soldier but was too afraid to go out into the fire.

When the gunshots calmed down, he peeped out to look for insurgents to aim for. He saw one man running and shot at him. After waiting another minute, he got up to find a total of six more men to aim at. Before he could get back to cover, he spotted a little boy who looked to be about nine years old walking his way. The boy was holding a 9mm pistol and shooting towards Jamaal. Jamaal's heart was racing as he could not bring himself to shoot the boy. Then another soldier came from around the corner spraying four rounds into the little boy's torso.

At that point Jamaal was traumatized and so hurt. After about two hours of shooting and scavenging the village, Jamaal's crew had suffered ten deaths and twenty-one injured soldiers. The soldier he saw get shot in the neck survived the hit but was in critical condition. In Jamaal's mind, this was not a victory. They had killed eighteen children, two women, and thirty-three men. There were many more people in the village, but they did not intentionally harm those who did not pose a threat to them. He could not wrap his mind around what had happened. The surviving people in the village looked terrified of them. Jamaal wondered why they looked so terrified if they were coming in to save the people. After that day, Jamaal was never the same.

Jamaal found himself staring out the window for another thirty minutes until he decided to make his way back to bed. Sleep never came easy, but he managed to doze off briefly after he laid back down. The next morning, he woke up to the smell of eggs, bacon, cheese grits, and blueberry pancakes. His mom loved to cook, and he definitely loved eating her food.

He threw a shirt on and went downstairs to greet his mom. "Good morning, Mama." Jamaal gave his mom a hug and kiss on the cheek.

"Good morning baby, you came down just in time. Everything is all done." She started to fix his plate as he poured a glass of orange juice. "I heard you downstairs in the middle of the night. Is everything okay with you?" she asked in a very concerned manner. She knew that her son had been through a lot and wanted to support him the best way that she could.

Jamaal let out a long sigh before he responded, "To be honest Mama, everything is not okay, and life will never be the same. I woke up frantically because of the fireworks outside, but in my mind, I thought they were gunshots. Hearing that noise made me feel like I was back in Iraq. It's very hard for me to get sleep these days thinking about everything that happened, and loud sounds stress me out even more."

His mom placed the food in front of him, along with syrup, salt, and pepper. "Baby, I know you have been through a lot. I truly thank God every day that you are still here with us. I know there isn't anything that I can say or do to erase the trauma that you have faced. I really want to encourage you to go speak to somebody. I hear people talk about their war stories and how their post-traumatic stress disorder has caused them to lose everything. I don't want to lose you, and I want you to be able to move on with your life one day." They hugged and proceeded to eat their breakfast.

Later that day Jamaal called Jakeshia to catch up on things. "Keshia, what's going on baby girl? I've been meaning to call you since I got back in town, but I have a lot going on." Jamaal was a little nervous because deep down he'd always had a huge crush on her.

"Hey Jamaal! It's all good, I really should've called you to check on you. I've been a bad friend. Let's meet up to grab some lunch today!" Jakeshia was excited and hoped that he was available.

"Cool, where would you like to meet?" Jamaal got up and started to look for clothes to throw on.

"How about I come scoop you in an hour and we head to Tin Lizzy's. I have a craving for their tortilla chips." She burst out laughing, because who really had a craving for tortilla chips? But Tin Lizzy's did season the hell out of them.

"Bet, I'll be ready in an hour." They both hung up to get ready.

Jamaal ran outside to hop in the car with Jakeshia. She was bumping Usher's Confessions album, and they both started to sing. "It's the simple things in life we forget, you hear her talking but don't hear what she says." They hugged as they laughed at their horrible duet. Jamaal couldn't think of a person on Earth who couldn't recite every lyric from every song on the Confessions album. Usher really put his heart and soul into that album. You could tell that he had done some dirt and it weighed heavy on him, guess he finally couldn't face the man that was staring at him in the mirror.

"Woman, I love that album!" Jamaal told Jakeshia as he turned the volume up.

"Man, me too, Mal. Usher was one scandalous ass dude! You know the girls and I were able to personally meet him the last time that I saw you. He called me up to the stage at Primetime, and I actually got to dance with him. And check this out... he invited me to go to a party that was at Justin Timberlake's house! Jamaal, I had such an amazing time that night. I really wish you could have made it out with us." Jakeshia was smiling from ear to ear as she reminisced about everything that happened that night, including the wet dream she almost had.

"Dang girl, that's what's up. I really wish I could've made it out that night too, but I'm really not myself. I have so much to say but just don't even know how to really express everything that's going on in my heart and head. Jakeshia, I'm so fucked up right now." Jamaal hung his head and wanted to cry but held himself together.

"Damn J, I'm so sorry to hear that you aren't in the best place. Don't ever forget that I am always here for you if you need anything. I mean that." Jakeshia grabbed his hand.

"Thank you, I really appreciate you. I'm going to try my best to open up, there's just so many things I need to say." They rode the rest of the way to the restaurant in silence. They arrived at Tin Lizzy's and decided to get a table in the back. They ordered a side of guacamole, fish tacos, chicken tacos, veggies nachos, and veggies tacos.

"So, I know I haven't really reached out lately, and I feel super bad about that. What is going on with you, friend?" Jakeshia asked.

"You're fine, I know you have your own thing going on right now with school and work. Jakeshia, the shit there was so bad." Jamaal began to tell Jakeshia about his first assignment in Iraq and how he felt like they killed a bunch of innocent people in the village. "After the first assignment, I just felt worthless. I couldn't believe that I had gotten fooled into being a bad guy. At that point I knew I wouldn't return once I was released.

"My second assignment was even worse than the first. We took a month off and just patrolled different areas to ensure that people were safe, had food, and clean water. When we were assigned this time, we had to go to the desert where insurgents were located. We were in camouflage and staked out the place for three days before we attacked. It was early in the morning, shortly before dawn. We started by creeping up with night goggles on. Two men at a time went up to find cover.

"Once we received the cue, we began to shoot at all targets in sight, it didn't matter if they were armed or not. I was timid but did as I was told. After an hour of shooting, stabbing, and searching, we had managed to kill everyone in that deserted area. Jakeshia, I really didn't understand any of this, and it hurt me to my core to see all of those people die." They sat in silence for a second as Jakeshia digested everything she had heard.

"Jamaal, I don't want you to blame yourself for any of the

choices you made during your time in the army. It really sounds like they were not transparent with any of you and had you all completing assignments without any truthful information. I am so sorry that you went through this, and I'm glad that you made it back to us safely." The food arrived and they dug in, making small talk in between bites. "So, if you're okay with talking about it. Could you finish telling me about your experience in Iraq? If you've spoken enough for the day, I totally understand." Jakeshia wanted her friend to be comfortable talking to her, but also didn't want to overwhelm him.

"I think I'm okay with sharing some more. So, after the second attack in the desert, I was active for five more assignments before my injury. Those assignments were similar to the first two. We went in and killed everyone in sight. It seemed like the more assignments we did, the more soldiers came back injured or killed. I think it's because we were all emotionally and physically drained. I had lost so many new friends and became paranoid believing that I would be the next soldier killed.

"My final assignment was in Baghdad. We were directed to go in and meet with one of the city leaders. Everything was going fine until this lady came in hysterical. She was screaming and crying while holding her head. We tried to calm her down, but one of the guards hit her in the back of the head with his gun. After the assault they dragged her body out of the room, and we didn't hear anything else about it. We asked the leader what was going on, but he changed the topic. We told the leader that we had to leave and report back to our captain. We could not witness an assault and stay there without knowing what was going on.

"Once we left, two of the guards followed us out and spit on us. My captain saw what happened and immediately became furious. Our goal was to reach a peace treaty for two of the leaders in Baghdad. My captain and five army men went back into the city to find out what happened to the lady and to get an apology from the guards that spit at us. When my captain returned, it was obvious that he was even more upset than when he left. He told us that the lady was upset because someone had killed her son the night before. Instead of helping the lady and sympathizing with her pain, they hit her and imprisoned her. To add to this, they did not apologize for spitting on us and further disrespected us. They threatened to bomb us all if the captain didn't leave his office.

"I don't know if it was protocol or if my captain was upset, but he ordered us to gear up. At this point I was confused but did as I was told. Jakeshia, I've never been so lost in my entire life. About an hour later, we stormed the place and shot at any armed individual we saw. After I shot seven people, I felt this strong burning feeling on my face and before I knew it, I had passed out. When I woke up, I had an IV in my arm, I was lying in a bed, and I could not feel my face. I had gotten shot in my jaw while on a mission that I didn't even know the purpose of. I felt so useless, so worthless, so invaluable in that moment. If I would've died that day, it would have been depicted that I died fighting for my country. Truth is, I don't know what the hell I was fighting for!" Jamaal shed tears of sorrow and joy. He was sad that he had been injured in the battle but grateful to have come out of it with his life.

"Jamaal, it breaks my heart to hear about your experiences. I really appreciate you sharing this with me. I know it takes a lot to talk about these things while you are so emotionally hurt. I do want you to know that I admire your strength. I am here whenever you need me. I know it sounds redundant but sometimes we forget that we are not alone." Jakeshia got up and gave Jamaal a hug. She could not believe all of these things that her friend was holding onto all this time. All she could think about was how everyone was fighting their own battles that they did not talk about.

When she saw Jamaal the other week, he did not look like this broken man. Aside from his facial scars, he appeared to be his regular self. Jakeshia wished there was more that she could do, but she knew it would take time and lots of counseling to heal these wounds. They continued to eat and started talking about the past. "Jakeshia, you know I had the biggest crush on you in school." Jamaal grinned as he ate a chip with dip.

"Whaaat? No, I had no idea. I always thought we were just really good buddies. We were such close friends within our circle, I've always looked at you like a brother, you know." Jakeshia was baffled that Jamaal was expressing himself. They went way back and were a part of the same friend circle. She couldn't understand why he was expressing himself at this moment. She didn't want to overlook his statement or be too nonchalant, but she could never see a future with Jamaal.

"Are you about ready to head out of here? I know you must have some schoolwork or something to complete." Jamaal looked exhausted, and he honestly felt awkward after telling Jakeshia how he felt in the past. But really who was he kidding? After seeing Jakeshia, all of those feelings had resurfaced. He knew by her response that there wasn't a chance in hell that he would ever bag her. He was definitely in the friend zone for life, but why even ruin a solid friendship like theirs? Plus, he was an emotional wreck after everything he had experienced in the service.

"Yeah, you're right, I do have tons of work to do so I can finish the last half of the semester off right." They paid their bill and hopped in the car to head back to Lithonia.

They sat the entire car ride in silence. Jamaal was emotionally exhausted, and Jakeshia did not know what to say. Not only was she hurting for her friend, but she was also taken aback by his confession. That lunch outing definitely left her with mixed emotions. Jamaal on the other hand felt like a complete fool. He shouldn't have told her how he felt, because truth be told the feelings he had never went away. "Well, we're here. I really enjoyed spending time with you. We must do it again with the old crew." Jakeshia looked over at him and smiled cheerfully.

"Yes, we must. I do miss everyone. In due time I'll be ready to kick it." They hugged and went their separate ways.

Jamaal walked in the house and asked his mom for the yellow pages. At that point he was determined to speak to a psychologist. One of the members at veteran affairs suggested that he start seeing a psychiatrist for his PTSD, but he'd be a damn fool to resort to drugs for treatment instead of just talking through it all. Living in metro Atlanta, he had seen so many people resort to drugs as a coping mechanism. You had the old heads who did crack and cocaine back in the 80's. Some of these folks were functional drug addicts, but then you had the people who were just strung out on drugs.

He absolutely understood that life stressed people out and drove them insane, but he never understood how some abandoned their entire life, including kids, just to get high all day. The people doing drugs nowadays popped pills of all sorts, drank promethazine, and drank codeine. He had seen these different cocktails make people wild, sluggish, and abusive.

Although drug abuse and drug use were two totally different things, he did not want to develop an addiction to any type of prescription drug. A psychologist was the best route at the moment. He found a local doctor in the area, a young black educated man who graduated from Morehouse. He immediately called Dr. Vaughn Gay's office to set up a meeting. Today was his lucky day, as Dr. G was able to schedule him for the next morning. Jamaal was nervous but so excited for this new journey. It was crazy how six months in the army had changed his entire life; he just wanted to feel normal again.

The next morning, Jamaal woke up to his mom's famous omelets and a waffle. He ate his breakfast as quickly as possible, since he didn't want to be late for his first therapy session. Once finished, he brushed his teeth, washed his face, got dressed, and took off in his moms' car. Jamaal hadn't purchased a vehicle since he had been away in the military, but he had plans to get one real soon. He only had a ten-minute drive to the Stonecrest mall area, as the office was in one of the nearby plazas. He parked and started walking towards the building with sweaty palms and a knot in his stomach.

Dr. G greeted him once he walked into the office. The waiting room decor was very soothing. There was a mini-waterfall, pictures of the ocean, soulful jazz playing, and an aromatherapy candle burning. This doctor really knew how to set a calming mood for his clients, Jamaal thought to himself. "Hi, Jamaal, I'm Dr. Vaughn Gay. It's my pleasure meeting you." Dr. G extended his hand for a handshake.

"Nice meeting you Dr. G. I appreciate you squeezing me into your schedule so soon." Jamaal shook his hand in return.

"My pleasure, brother. I had this opening, so it's only right that we start your day off on the right path. Come follow me into the liberation room." Jamaal followed Dr. G, and once he entered the room, he understood why the room was named the 'liberation room'. The vibe was so free and embodied pure tranquility. The walls were painted two tones, which included ocean blue and a light gray. The furniture was spaced out and a neutral gray with various shades of blue around the room. There was a collection of plants that were near the window soaking up the natural sunlight. The air purifier was going along with an essential oil diffuser. He also had some smooth jazz playing in the background. This office reminded him of what home should feel like.

"I'm really digging this room. It's really chill in here." Jamaal couldn't help but look around in amazement. He wasn't one for decor, but this room really made him feel a little more at peace.

"Thanks man, I really have to give all of the praise to my wonderful wife. She designed my entire office space. I handed her my business card and she made it all happen on a budget. You can choose any seat that you'd like, I don't have a specific chair. I want you to be as comfortable as possible." Dr. G waited on Jamaal, then he took a seat.

"Thank you, doc. This seat is quite comfortable." Jamaal was seated on a chaise that allowed him to extend his legs to fully relax.

"You're welcome brother. I want our sessions to be productive. So, I'm going to start by asking you some preliminary questions." Dr. G went on to ask Jamaal his age, his current living environment, and other personal information.

"I'm nineteen, I have lived in the suburban area of Lithonia for most of my life with my beautiful mother, my dad was in and out of the picture, and I've pretty much spent the first part of my adulthood training for and in the military." Jamaal started to get nervous again as he anticipated the eye-opening questions that were on the way. He didn't mind spilling his guts about his life if that's what it took for him to feel somewhat normal again. He took a deep breath and braced himself for the remainder of his hour.

Dr. G continued to ask questions so he could get an idea of Jamaal's life from childhood to the present. As a counselor, he always encouraged his clients to unpack their life and be transparent. He knew that one could not be effectively treated without knowing the essential details of who they were, where they came from, where they wished to be, and who they aimed to be. Each individual was different, and their needs varied. "So, you mentioned that your dad was in and out of your life. Are there special circumstances that kept him away? Did his absence have a negative or positive impact on you?" Dr. G had placed his glasses back on his face and prepared to take notes.

"That's a heavy set of questions." Jamaal chuckled before giving it all he had. "So apparently my dad had an entirely different family. He and my mom were at a bar one night when they met, and he wasn't wearing his wedding ring. They kicked it off, exchanged numbers, and he insisted on meeting up for breakfast the next day. They went for breakfast at a diner in Sandy Springs and the rest was history. About two months into their so-called relationship, I was conceived. Once my mom told him she was pregnant, everything changed. She didn't find out about his wife until she was seven months pregnant and preparing for the baby shower.

"He finally appeared with his wedding ring on his finger. He claimed that he and his wife were separated when my parents first met, but they had gotten back together a week later. He was too enticed by my mom to tell her the truth. So cowardly and manipulative. Once my mom found out about his wife, she didn't want much to do with him. She insisted that he could not have a close relationship with me as long as he kept up the lies. To this day he never told his wife that I existed. I don't know much about him or my stepmom. Whenever he came around, we would just talk about whatever I had going on in that moment of life. His visits never lasted long. I haven't seen him since I enlisted in the army. It would've been great to have grown up with an active, loving father. Instead, I had a lying, prideful asshole who helped create me. I honestly don't know what role his absence played in my life. My mom did the best she could, and I think I turned out pretty alright."

Jamaal cracked a smile through his tears. He didn't expect to go full Justin Timberlake and cry a river, but he felt a sense of relief to finally speak about the feelings he had toward his sperm donor. "Thank you for sharing that with me. As black men, it is very challenging for us to express our emotions, and you laid it all out on the table with no holding back. I appreciate you for trusting me and feeling comfortable enough to be vulnerable. This is a safe space, and I intend on getting you through this process with more clarity and personal growth." Dr. G went on to tell his experiences with his father growing up.

He grew up in the late 70s and early 80s and had an unconventional relationship with his dad as well. After Dr. G spoke about his childhood, Jamaal felt even more relieved. It was comforting to know that there were other men he could relate to. Growing up in a household where your mom was the sole provider and nurturer had its challenges, but these two men seemed to be successful. Although Jamaal was still very young and just getting started; he had graduated high school with a 3.5 grade point average, played multiple sports, was a complete gentleman to the ladies, and a great friend. He analyzed all of these things and looked at Dr. G, and for the first time in his life, he was truly appreciative of growing up without a consistent father.

Five

Chapter 5

Jakeshia was so tired by the time she got home from lunch with Jamaal. It was true what they said about being emotionally drained. She immediately took a shower and put on some night clothes to get comfortable. She went to the kitchen to make tea while she read a few chapters for school. Her phone rang, and it was her mom. They didn't talk often because Jacqueline wasn't very social. "Hey Ma, what's going on?" Jakeshia was in a studying groove, so she was being short.

"Hey, I was calling to tell you that your brother got locked up early this morning." She let out a sign, and Jakeshia knew her mom was shaking her head.

"What did he do this time? The boy hasn't learned his lesson?" Jakeshia didn't have an ounce of sympathy to give, considering for the past nine years, she couldn't recall a year that Raquan went without getting locked up.

"He is being charged with a lot this time. Apparently, he and

50

three other people drove out to Winder, Georgia to commit armed robbery. According to the police report, they arrived at a couple's house late in the evening, approached the husband with a gun outside, hit him in the back of his head with the gun, and went inside. Once they were inside, they tied up the man and his wife and asked them where all of their valuables were. They raided their house and got away with over $10,000 in cash and other possessions that were valued close to $100,000."

Jakeshia had to stop her mom mid-sentence. "How did they even know that these people owned any of this stuff, or would even have that much cash laying around the house?" She was really baffled and knew it couldn't be a coincidence.

"One of the people who was with Raquan used to work with their daughter. But let me finish. So, they left the house and kept the people tied up and on their way back to the city they got a flat tire on the interstate. The state patrol saw them and stopped. As soon as they saw the state patrol, they closed the trunk and started to act suspiciously. The officer and his partner approached the vehicle and asked a few questions. The guy told the officers that they were heading back home from North Carolina when they caught a flat tire on 85 north. At that exact moment, the officers received a radio call about a vehicle matching the same description. The officers called for backup and ordered everyone to show their hands."

Jakeshia stopped her mom. "Wait, hold up! How do you know every single detail? Were you there?" Jakeshia laughed as she looked up at the clock. It was now a quarter past 7 and she was exhausted.

"All of this was in the police report, smarty pants. But anyways, the remaining passengers were then ordered to get out of the vehicle. Since they were outnumbered, they cuffed everyone. The guy who was outside changing the tire asked the officer if they were under arrest and if it was against their rights to be cuffed. The officer insisted that they were not under arrest, but they had a suspicion that the vehicle was a part of criminal activity so they had the right to search the vehicle. Girl, they popped the trunk and saw everything that was missing from those people's house, minus the cash, of course. They radioed the other officers who were reporting to inform them what they found, then proceeded to search the remainder of the car. Once inside the car, they found a shotgun, two 9mm, and a Taurus .38 handgun. They knew they were in trouble then. One of the officers asked why they were traveling back in state with all of those firearms. North Carolina was a state where guns are allowed, but of course they were trying to get the full story.

"So apparently your brother spoke up and said they had the guns with them for protection and they were all legal. The officers then decided to search all four of the passengers. Girl, they found over $2,000 in each of their pockets, some cocaine, and marijuana. The one thing no one had on them was an ID or license. The officers then asked for them to tell the truth about where all those items came from, and what they were doing with drugs and that much money. No one spoke up. And that is pretty much everything so far. It's crazy how you can go commit a crime like that and then get a flat tire." Jakeshia was pretty much over it at this point. She didn't understand how she and her brother chose two totally opposite paths. They shared the same blood and grew up in the same household. But hey, everyone made their own decisions.

"Dang Ma, well keep me posted. I'm about to call it a night. I went to lunch with Jamaal earlier and I'm extremely tired." She yawned as she walked towards her room.

"Okay, tell Jamaal I said hey." They said their goodbyes then hung up. Jakeshia rarely went to sleep this early, but today was the day. She laid down for about five minutes then dozed off.

Jakeshia woke up at 7:47 a.m. to Teresa and Mya arguing. *What in the hell could they possibly be arguing about this early in the damn morning?* she asked herself as she went to wash her face and brush her teeth, then headed to the kitchen. "What the hell are y'all arguing about this fucking early in the morning?" Jakeshia asked as she went to grab a banana.

"This bitch always got some slick shit to say!" Mya was angrily pointing at Teresa.

Jakeshia chuckled before she responded, "Mya what the hell did you do now? You know your ass does not like accountability." Teresa agreed with Jakeshia.

"Girl, fuck both of y'all hoes!" Mya rolled her eyes as she went to go sit on the couch.

"Okay, but you didn't answer my question. Let me rephrase myself. What is the problem? Why is Teresa minding your business, girl?" Jakeshia asked, being serious and sarcastic at the same time.

"Y'all really do get on my nerves. So, the guy I met last week wants me to help him get a car by putting it in my name. Now before you say anything, he is going to pay for everything. He just needs me to put it in my name." Mya knew she was about to get a mouthful.

"Girl, what the fuck?! Teresa has the right to be getting on you! You just met this dude last week, how is it even a discussion? Tell his scrub ass to kick rocks. You better not even give him the idea that he can play with you like that!" Jakeshia was hot. Why the hell would Mya even be considering putting something in her name for a dude she had just met? She loved her friend, but she had some serious issues. You didn't finance things in your name for anyone, and damn sure not a stranger.

"Aw man, now here you go. I just got to arguing with Teresa about this mess. I don't have time to hear your mouth either, Keshia!" Mya snapped.

"Girl, that's all I honestly have to say. If you're dumb enough to let a complete stranger bamboozle your ass into getting them a car, then sis, that's on you." Jakeshia rolled her eyes and fixed her tea.

"What would make y'all think that I'm actually going to get a car in my name though. All I did was tell Teresa that the dude asked me to get the car. I never even told you my response. You just flew into a rant about me being stupid and gullible. For y'alls information, I told him that I don't know him well enough to get anything in my name for him. I don't even trust him enough to meet him in a private place right now." Mya was yelling and was totally offended that her best friends thought so little of her ability to make good choices. She knew she didn't always do the best things in life, but she was learning and growing. Young people made mistakes, but that was a part of life.

"Well, I apologize. I walked into y'alls argument thinking that you had agreed to get the car in your name. Teresa, you should have let her finish telling her story before you assumed she went along with the mess." Jakeshia was always the glue to the friendship, the voice of reason, and typically the calm one.

"Well, I'm sorry I assumed the worst." Teresa went over to give Mya a hug, but she shrugged her off. Mya was not feeling her friend's apology at the moment. She was truly offended.

"Well damn, fuck you too." Teresa was salty

"You pretty much said fuck me when you had an entire argument with me about nothing. Your raggedy ass doesn't deserve a golden hug from me." Mya burst out laughing as she walked back to her room.

Jakeshia finished getting herself together and headed to campus. She didn't eat breakfast that morning, as she didn't have much of an appetite. The news she had gotten from her mother the night before had her feeling anxious. She didn't agree with her brother's poor decisions but did not wish any bad to happen to him. She couldn't believe that he had landed his ass back into some more trouble. As she went out the door, her phone rang. She was hoping that it wouldn't be any more bad news. She let out a sigh of relief when she saw Michael's name appear on the screen.

"Good morning handsome, how are you doing today?" She was smiling hard already. She knew this conversation would be some relief from the emotional day she had yesterday and the crazy morning she'd woke up to.

"Hey gorgeous, I'm great now that I have you on the phone. What are you doing today?" Michael asked.

"I'm headed to campus now for a few classes and should be done close to three. Nothing planned after that." Jakeshia hopped in her car and headed downtown.

"Cool, I have a few classes myself. I wanted to see if we could link for dinner tonight. I know it's last minute, but one of my brothers is having this dinner party at Loca Luna in Brookhaven. I want you to be my date." Jakeshia wasn't expecting to be asked out and definitely was not expecting to meet any of his friends.

"Um, sure, that sounds like a fun time. What's the dress code?" She was a little nervous but wanted to make sure she made a good impression.

"Dress grown and sexy. I can't wait to see you later. I would ask to pick you up, but I remembered that you like to get to know people better before they know exactly where you live." Jakeshia got a little tingle in her chest. She loved how Michael was attentive and thoughtful.

"Thank you for always being respectful. Other dudes would've let that information go in one ear and out the other and tried to force it. But you, as always, are a true gentleman." They chatted some more on the phone until Jakeshia made it to Spelman campus. They said their goodbyes and promised to meet up around 7 p.m. that night in the Loca Luna parking lot.

Jakeshia was leaving her last class heading to her car when she heard a loud *BOOM* behind her. The noise startled her so bad that she missed a step and fell to the ground. A few seconds later, she heard another *BOOM!* At that point, she didn't know what the sound was nor where it was coming from, but her speculations led her to believe it was an explosion or gunshot. When she got up from the ground, she ran to hide inside the science building. She was frantic, and one of the security officers ordered everyone to head to the basement of the building. Jakeshia did as she was told, but she did not know what was going on but wanted to stay safe.

While in the basement, she saw students and staff members crying hysterically. A lady yelled out, "God please help us, please keep us safe. Lord, it is not my time to go!" Jakeshia started to cry. Those words were so real and made her feel as though everyone was in immediate danger. She did not know what to expect. After being in the basement for twenty-five minutes, everything settled down inside and outside the building. The security officer told everyone to hold tight as he made a call to his supervisor.

After a short conversation, the officer was directed to escort everyone out of the building. There had been a chemical explosion in one of the other science buildings. There were a few injuries, but so far, no fatalities. Jakeshia was relieved to know that there was not an immediate threat to herself and others. She hated the thought that anyone would be on campus trying to harm students and staff members. By then it was close to four p.m., and she knew she needed to get home and get ready for her date with Michael.

Jakeshia made it home around 4:40 p.m. Lucky for her there wasn't much traffic getting home. As soon as she walked through the door, Mya and Teresa rallied around her with hugs. "Girl, are you okay?! We've been trying to call you since we heard about the chemical explosion! Why haven't you answered us or called us back?" Teresa and Mya were so upset. They didn't know whether Jakeshia was safe or one of the individuals hurt.

"I'm sorry y'all. I was in the science building next to the explosion, so I was freaking out. My phone was in my book bag, and I was not thinking about anything but surviving. We didn't know what was going on. When it happened, we thought it was gunshots or a bombing. I was outside and ran into the science building where the security officer then rushed me into the basement. Y'all, there was about fifty of us down there. People were screaming, crying, and just plain old scared. We were there for about twenty-five minutes before we got clearance to leave. I've never been so terrified in my life." Jakeshia finally let it all out and started crying. The girls hugged her harder until she let go.

"Now I have to get ready for this date with my prince charming. I'll be damned if I let that scary situation disrupt the plans I have with a real man." Jakeshia smiled and wiped her face.

"Oh, so you have a date with that wonderful mystery guy Michael? Well, when will we get to sit down with him and pick his brain?" Teresa asked as if she was somebody's mama.

"Girl, I'm still getting to know him. This is only our second date, dang." Jakeshia sucked her teeth. "We know it's only the second date, but y'all sit on the damn phone all damn day. It's like we never get any time with you anymore between you being a manager at Arizona's, an honor student, and a wife!" Mya burst out laughing.

"Girl bye, far from a wife. Hell, I'm not even a girlfriend yet. But hey, if he continues to move like this, then I'm all in." Jakeshia slapped five with her girls then went to her room to get ready. She ransacked her closet looking for the most perfect outfit. She couldn't decide if she wanted to wear a dress, or some fitted pants with a cute top. She ultimately decided to wear some pants with a cute top since she was going to a tapas restaurant opposed to a bar or club. She hopped in the shower and lathered up with her dove body wash. Once she got out, she moisturized her body with the Bahamas passion fruit and banana flower shea body cream from Bath and Body Works. She felt like such a fucking lady!

She jumped into her hip hugging jeans and put on her off the shoulder blouse. She decided to accessorize with some silver hoop earrings, her silver necklace which carried her dove pendant, and a few silver bangles. Although she had on her lotion, she decided to pair it with her Marc Jacob's perfume to ramp up her floral smell. Jakeshia threw on her silver, shiny Jessica Simpson heels and took a look in the mirror. "Damn, I'm one fine ass woman!" she said out loud to herself. She put on some red lipstick, grabbed her purse and keys, and headed out the door.

When she got in her car, she called Michael to let him know she was on her way. She had three missed calls from him and a voicemail earlier. She knew he must've been calling to make sure she was safe, but it totally slipped her mind to give him a call back. "Hey handsome, I'm so sorry I didn't answer or return your call earlier." she said with a smile as she thought about what a beautiful chocolate king he was.

"Yeah love, I was calling because I heard there was an explosion at Spelman today. I was so worried and wanted to make sure you were safe. I'm so glad you called me. How are you?" Michael sounded so concerned.

"I'm good, thank you for checking in on me. I was actually near the building right next to the explosion. I didn't know if it was gunshots, a bomb going off or what. I was super scared but relieved when I found out there weren't any casualties. But on to something positive, I'm on my way to Loca Luna to see you." She was smiling again.

"Damn, after the day you had you still heading my way? I must be the luckiest man alive!" Michael chuckled a little, and she could tell that he was blushing through the phone.

"I have absolutely been looking forward to seeing you. I should be there in about thirty minutes." They said their goodbyes and hung up the phone. Jakeshia vibed to some Erykah Badu for the rest of her ride.

Jakeshia arrived at Loca Luna around 6:57 p.m. She tried her best to always be on time, she refused to be on colored people time. Sometimes it was okay to be fashionably late, but she had too much respect for Michael to be late when conditions allowed her to be there. She gave Michael a call to let him know she'd arrived. He was pulling in, so she decided to get out of her car and wait for him on the sidewalk. The area was live. The music from Loca Luna and The Old Blind Dog had the block hot. The people she saw walking to the different businesses looked happy and high off life.

Although her afternoon was rough, she was convinced that the rest of her night would be one for the books. Michael walked towards her and looked delighted to see her. All she could think about was how good he looked in his Tommy Hilfiger outfit. Unlike a lot of the guys around the way, Michael had his pants on his waist and they weren't too baggy. These days it was rare to see a brother who wasn't sagging his pants trying to show off his boxers or briefs. She never understood why any dudes wore their pants below their ass, considering the fact that the trend was started in the prisons as an indication that the men were gay and available. At least that's what the word on the streets was. Either way, the shit was ugly. Nobody wanted to see a man's ass nor his draws.

She was so impressed by Michael's choice of clothing, and he smelled so good. They greeted each other and hugged, and she damn near melted in his arms. Whew, she had some thoughts running through her head. "You smell really nice Michael, what cologne is that?" she asked with a smile.

"I had to shop black on this one, beautiful. This is that Sean John's Unforgivable. But I swear I'll forgive you every time." They both burst out laughing. There's nothing like a corny play on words. "You look stunning Jakeshia, and smell like some edible arrangements if I might add. I didn't know you were going to step out like this. I should've put on my suit and tie to match your beauty." Michael always had the compliments. They chatted briefly to catch up on the day's events and went into Loca Luna to meet his brothers.

"Ayyye it's the life of the party! You can find me in the club, a bottle full of bub mama, I got what you need if you need to feel the buzz!" Some random guy walked up on them and started to rap to 50 Cents' 'In Da Club' as it played. Michael and the guy hugged, then Michael introduced the guy as Joe.

"Hi Joe, it's nice to meet you." He gave her a hug and offered her a drink. They had bottles at their table filled with different brown and white liquors, champagne, and wine. Jakeshia declined a drink since she needed to get some food in her stomach. Michael escorted her around and introduced her to a few other guys and girls before they sat down to order food. She grabbed a menu and didn't hesitate to order multiple items. After all, tapas were small portions of food.

She ordered the fried calamari with a sweet chili sauce, a vegetarian chile relleno, shrimp cocktail, and a salmon roll. Michael looked at her and smiled at the fact that she showed no mercy on the menu. "Okay, I like a woman who knows how to eat. Can I have some of your food when it comes?" Michael was grinning from ear to ear.

"A girl's gotta eat, you know. And you sure can. I don't mind sharing, as long as you do the same." Jakeshia chuckled as one of her favorite songs came on. The song 'Yeah' by Usher featuring Lil' Jon and Ludacris started to play. She got up and started swaying her hips to the beat. That song was for sure a club banger and meant so much more to her since she had met

Usher a few weeks ago. Michael stood up next to her and started bopping from side to side. They made eye contact and smiled at each other. The next song that played was Sean Paul's 'I'm still in love with you'. They both went with the vibe of the song and started to dance together. The reggae song evoked a lot of winding from the hips.

Jakeshia got close to Michael and danced. He slipped his arm around her and placed it at the small of her back. They both whined and grind like no one was watching. Jakeshia was getting a little hot, at least dancing that close to Michael made her a little overwhelmed. When the song stopped playing, she sat down to have a sip of water. She didn't want to get too carried away with him just yet, after all they were still getting to know each other. Moments later, their food arrived, and it looked amazing. They both dug into their individual plates. As promised, they shared their food and enjoyed it all. Once they finished eating, they had a few drinks of wine.

Jakeshia just wanted something to take her mind off of the events from earlier that day. The wine mellowed her and then she got up to mingle and dance some more. They stayed there and partied until close to 1 a.m. when they decided to call it a night. Michael walked Jakeshia to her car, and they kissed for the first time. At that moment, there were hundreds of fireworks going off, in Jakeshia's head of course. They said their goodbyes then went their separate ways.

Jakeshia arrived home at 1:30 a.m. and took a quick shower. She was on cloud nine after the night she had but couldn't sit up too long gloating since she had work in a few hours. She was able to drift off to sleep shortly after she laid down and had the most amazing dream about her and Michael. Jakeshia dreamed that they lived in Miami, Florida alongside the beach with the best view of the Atlantic Ocean. She was pregnant and expecting their first child.

BUZZZZZZ! Jakeshia's alarm went off to wake her for work. "UGH!" she screamed. She was so tired from school and her night with Michael. She did not want to work, but how else was she going to maintain her portion of the bills? She dragged herself out of bed around 7:05 a.m. to go brush her teeth and wash her face. She got dressed, grabbed a banana, and headed out the door. She had to be at work by 7:45 a.m. so she could open up for the prep cooks and create the floor chart for the day.

She made it to work on time and went straight to the kitchen to make herself and the two employees some green tea. She always kept tea and honey at work for early mornings and late nights. Today she had to be at work for a ten-hour shift, so she would need all the energy she could possibly get. Once the tea was finished, she fixed her mug with a teaspoon of honey and a lemon wedge.

"Thank you, Ms. Jakeshia, you always take care of us. I'm so happy that you got your promotion, you're so sweet and really know the business." The female prep cook was like a mother figure to Jakeshia while at work. They always helped each other out, and she always brought Jakeshia home cooked meals. Her Cajun pasta was a fan favorite! Mrs. Nancy always used jumbo shrimp, blackened salmon, a cashew cream sauce, and fettuccine. The staff was really going to make it hard for Jakeshia to leave when she graduated from college. "You're welcome Mama Nancy. You always take care of me, so I must return the favor. You all work so hard and are always here when I need you." They gave each other a hug and went to do their respective jobs.

While Jakeshia was in the office, her phone rang, and it was Raoul. She ignored the call and continued to create the seating charts for the servers. A few seconds later, her phone rang again, but she still was not going to answer. She was annoyed at the fact that he had the audacity to be calling her, especially so early in the morning. Her phone went off again to notify her that she had a voicemail message and a text message followed.

The text message was from Raoul and read, "Jakeshia I really really miss you. You don't understand how much I luv u. I no I made a lot of fuked up choices but I really want 2 be a betta person for u. I promise this if u give me anotha chance ill do u rite. Please call me bak. I luv u nd I miss u." After reading his text message, she listened to his whack ass voicemail.

"Baby, please answer the phone or call me back. I miss you. I'm so sorry. You know no other girl matters to me. It's always been you, and it will always be you. I don't know what's wrong with me. I need you in my life. I promise I'm done playing games. Jakeshia, I love you, and I promise I'm going to spend the rest of my life with you, girl. Call me back please!" Jakeshia laughed and shook her head at the messages. She was so over the apologies and fake ass 'I love you's. Raoul did this shit every time she left. She promised herself that last time was the last time for her to deal with his shit. She was young but refused to be categorized as dumb. She gave him enough chances and there was no way she was going to go back to that nonsense. She had a bright future ahead of her. She put her phone on silent since he continued to call her. He'd never been this persistent when she ignored him. He was coming off as narcissistic and obsessive.

Once she finished the seating chart and deep cleaning the hostess podium and windows, she decided to listen to the other voicemails he had left. "Baby I don't know why you are ignoring me like this. It's us forever. If I'm not with you then I don't want to be with anybody else. You're the best person I've ever had in my life. I swear there's no other person for me. Jakeshia, pick up the phone, dammit. This shit is getting out of hand. You got me over here going crazy. I'm really losing my mind. Please don't make me do it, I'll do it. If I can't have you there's no purpose for me being on this earth. You hear me, Jakeshia? I'll kill myself. Do you want that on your conscience?"

Jakeshia was so lost. She had never heard Raoul talk that insane. The dude was crazy, but what in the hell was he on today? He had called her phone over twenty times and left three voicemails. She decided to call him back so the madness could stop. "Raoul, stop calling my damn phone with this stupid shit! I am at work and you over here calling me like you don't have anything better to do. I am DONE with you. Get that through your thick skull. The last time was the last time. I don't even know what I ever saw in your clown ass in the first place. You are for the streets, and I am for a grown ass man. Don't call my phone anymore. Please have a wonderful day and take care!" She hung up the phone and didn't give him the opportunity to get a word in. In her eyes he had said enough through his text message and voicemails. Hopefully he got the picture that she wanted absolutely nothing to do with him.

A notification went off on her phone; it was Raoul sending a text message. "I really love u Keshia and I hope one day you will understand dat. I guess this is goodbye." She sighed in relief that he was done interrupting her day. She was finally able to focus with no interruptions as she had to go to the back and do inventory on all of the stocked food and beverages.

Jakeshia was more than halfway through a busy shift. All of her servers were there working hard, but a few were not meeting the demands of their customers. Arizona's was a very popular spot, and Saturdays were always packed to the max. She was running food and drinks to the table, pouring glasses of wine for the bartender, and even flipping a few steaks for the head chef. The other manager that was supposed to come that morning didn't make it to work due to an illness, so she was stuck by herself filling in all the missing pieces. It was a lot of work, but she didn't mind because she knew she would get paid more for working alone.

Once everything calmed down, she decided to go into the office to take a breather. She hadn't looked at her phone in a while, but once she looked there were tons of missed calls from various people. Raoul had called a million times, Teresa, Mya, and even Raoul's mom. She wondered what all these people had wanted with her today. It was unusual for all of these people to have called and left voicemails. She called Raoul's mom to see what she wanted. She never called Jakeshia when she knew they weren't dating. "Hey Ms. Martha, I see I have a missed call from you." Jakeshia spoke in a very nonchalant tone. She wanted this to be a quick and easy conversation.

Ms. Martha burst out crying hysterically. "HE SHOT HIMSELF IN THE HEAD! RAOUL SHOT HIMSELF!" Ms. Martha was screaming and crying.

"WHAT? Raoul shot himself?" Jakeshia asked frantically. She knew he was talking crazy on the phone, but she didn't expect him to do anything to harm himself.

"YES! He called me and told me that he loved me, and that he would see me in heaven. I asked him what was going on, but he hung up the phone on me. I rushed over to his place and walked into his room to see him lying unconscious on the floor with a gun in his hand. I called 911, and he still had a pulse. He's at Grady hospital and in critical condition. I couldn't sit up there, Jakeshia. I was driving myself crazy. I CAN'T LOSE MY BABY!" She started crying again.

"Oh my goodness, I spoke to him earlier and he was talking crazy. He said he couldn't live life without me, but I didn't expect him to do anything like this. I should've talked to him longer or called you. I'm so sorry this happened. Please keep me posted on his condition. I'm so sorry Ms. Martha." Jakeshia got off the phone with her and broke down crying. She loved Raoul and didn't want any harm to go his way. She couldn't believe that he had tried to commit suicide. Raoul was one of the toughest guys she knew. She couldn't focus on work anymore. She just sat in her office in a daze.

When she snapped out of the daze, she went to the office refrigerator to make herself a shot of Grey Goose. She never drank on the job, but she didn't see any other way she could finish up her shift. She wanted to leave work so bad, but she realized that there was nothing she could do about Raoul's condition. She could only pray and hope for the best outcome. If only she would've let him talk on the phone, maybe things would have turned out different.

Six

Raoul's Story

⁓⦉⦊⁓

"What's up baby, what you doing?" Raoul called Amber around midnight hoping to get him some late-night loving.

"Hey boo, I'm just chilling. Up, thinking about you." She sounded excited, so Raoul knew she would pull up to his place if he asked.

"Come over, I got something I want to show you. I know you miss this." They did a little more small talk, and five minutes later, Amber was on her way. While Raoul waited on Amber to arrive, he rolled up a blunt of kush. He lit his blunt then went to the kitchen to fix two shots of Hennessy. He knew exactly what Amber wanted to drink, and he loved having drunk sex with her.

A few minutes later, Amber knocked on the door. She didn't stay too far away. "Damn, come on in sexy." Amber was dressed in some extremely tight booty shorts with some thigh high boots on. All Raoul could think about was taking her to the bedroom and getting her undressed.

"Thank you bae, you're so sweet. I got dressed just for you. That ass sitting right, ain't it?" Amber smiled as she did a 360-degree turn.

"DAMN! You put that on for me?" Raoul bit his bottom lip, smacked Amber on the ass, and pulled her close to him. They kissed passionately for a few seconds before they sat down on the sofa. "Here, I poured you a shot of Hennessy." Raoul handed Amber her shot and then lit the blunt. He took a few puffs and passed the blunt to Amber.

"So what you get into yesterday?" Raoul asked Amber before he choked on the smoke from his blunt pull.

"You honestly won't guess how my day went. How about I saw that bitch Jakeshia at The Sundial today."

Raoul cut Amber off, "Hold up, hold up. Watch your mouth. Jakeshia ain't a bitch. You gotta calm all dat there down." Amber looked at Raoul sideways. She couldn't believe he was taking up for her.

"Anyways! I saw her at The Sundial today and she got real nasty with me. I don't know why you're taking up for her. She's always super rude to me when I see her. What's your problem? Why don't you ever take up for me like dat?" Amber stood up and was obviously upset at the moment.

"Girl, sit yo ass down. You know me and Jakeshia got history. Of course, she's going to have an attitude with you when I cheated on her with you. What you want her to be, your friend or somethin?" Raoul pulled Amber back down to sit down on his lap. He fixed another round of Hennessy shots and started to rub on her leg. "I don't want to hear about her anymore. I want to see what else that mouth can do besides talking." Raoul grinned as he placed his hand on the top of Amber's head to push it towards his genitals.

"Boy whatever, I'm mad at you. But I didn't come over here for nothing." Amber proceeded to pull down Raoul's pants to expose his rock-hard penis. She gently massaged it in clockwise and counterclockwise directions using both of her hands. One hand placed at the base and the other at the top. She looked up to Raoul to see him biting his bottom lip in excitement. That was all the fuel she needed to begin the real work of her blowjob. She slowly placed her mouth on the tip of his dick and began to rotate her head in circles. She moved her tongue in circles and up and down.

Next, she lowered her head even further, inviting his dick to meet her tonsils. She began to speed up the pace, still rotating her head, moving her tongue, and adding some cheek suctioning to the action. Raoul started to moan loudly as the sensations intensified. He still had his hand on her head going with the up and down motion of Amber's head. She was a real head doctor.

After three minutes of sucking, Raoul had ejaculated all in her mouth. He removed his dick and led her to his bedroom. His room was filthy with clothes, soda cans, beer bottles, and tobacco everywhere. Amber didn't care how unsanitary Raoul was, she just wanted a dude she could kick it with. He told her to get undressed as he threw all the clothes off his bed. He bent her over and rammed his dick into her vagina, showing her no mercy. She moaned loudly when he entered and immediately got wet. She loved it rough, and Raoul was never gentle with her.

He pounded her fast from behind and began to smack her butt while pulling her hair. She threw her butt back and moaned even louder. "Oh my god, Raoul why you doing this to me?"

Amber moaned as she got off beat from his thrusting.

"Shut up and take the dick!" Raoul yelled as he smacked her ass again. He began to go even harder as sweat dripped from his face and chest. After ten minutes of back action, he nutted on her back and butt. Amber continued to bend over the bed as Raoul went into the bathroom to get a warm rag to clean her up.

"Damn bae, you were amazing." Amber smiled and was on cloud nine after that session. She crawled into his bed and laid down while he went to roll up another blunt.

"So babe, when are we going to make this official now that ole girl is out of the picture?" Amber wanted Raoul to make her his girl. She had been dealing with him for over five years on and off. She couldn't believe that he had chosen Jakeshia instead of her over and over again.

"Listen, I told you I wasn't ready for all of dat. You keep pressing the issue. I don't even like dating for real. What we got going on is good to me. We kickin it, I feed you from time to time, and fuck you real good. You even said it's the best you eva had. Please stop tryin' to destroy what we got going on while it's good." Raoul got snappy. He really wasn't the relationship type. He had gotten with Jakeshia because she was sweet, motherly, supportive, ambitious, and drama free. It was funny that he hated drama but did so much to attract drama his way, now ain't that crazy?

"Wow! I'm over here madly in love with you. Fuckin and suckin you good. I haven't dealt with any other dudes lately, and you still don't want me!" Amber got up and got dressed.

"I do want you. I love everything we got going on, we good as is. Why complicate shit with a wack ass title?" Raoul hit his lit blunt as he kicked his feet up on the bed.

71

"Raoul, are you serious? I want you all to myself. Without that wack ass title, you're free to do whatever with whoever." She looked around for one of her earrings, rumbling through all of the clothes on his floor.

"And what's wrong with me dealing with other people? You had no problem fuckin' with me all this time while I was with Jakeshia. Now all of a sudden you want me all to yourself. That ain't what you signed up for, baby girl." Raoul chuckled as he shook his head.

"I stuck around hoping that one day you would leave her for me, seeing the value that I bring to your life." Amber's voice was getting shaky. She felt like a complete fool. Why the fuck was he laughing at her as if her feelings were a joke?

"I don't know why you would think I'd ever leave Jakeshia for a female like you. You're cool peoples and all, but what typa fuckin' value do you add to a playas life? See, some of y'all hoes hold yourself too fuckin high out here. You were willingly a side bitch. So be happy wheneva I'm fuckin' wit you. This dick and me are gold, ya hear me? Gold! If you not cool wit us as we are, I'm not kissin' your ass to make you stay. I fuck wit chu though." Raoul looked nonchalant as Amber continued to get dressed.

"I don't know why I played myself dealing with you. Why would I think you could ever want me and only me, and love me? I guess this is goodbye, Raoul. I want love, marriage, and a family one day." Amber walked out of his room expecting him to stop her, but he didn't. What a fool she had been, thinking that Raoul would commit to her. Most dudes couldn't see forever in a side chick, they just wanted someone to get away from reality with. Raoul got up unphased and went to go lock his front door. When he got back to his room, he thought about Jakeshia until he dozed off.

BOOM! BOOM! BOOM! BOOM! Raoul jumped up out of bed when he heard the banging at his from door. He grabbed his Taurus .38 handgun and went to look to see who it could be banging on his door like that. He looked out the peephole, but it was covered. He slowly walked to the window to discreetly peep out of the curtain. He let out a sigh of relief once he saw it was his homie, Bear. He put his pistol in his waistband and opened the door.

"Nigga, why you bangin' on my damn door like you the mothafuckin' police or somethin'?" Raoul gave Bear some dap then walked into the kitchen.

"Boy, shut yo ass up. You always crying and shit!" Bear was 6 feet 7 inches tall and husky. He was one of those dudes who should've played pro football but got caught up in the street life. "What you got to eat in this bitch?" Bear followed Raoul to the kitchen and began to raid the refrigerator.

"Nothing for yo ass. Why didn't you eat before you came over here? You interrupting my dream about fuckin' yo mama and didn't even eat before you got here!" Raoul started laughing at his joke, but Bear didn't find it funny and slapped him on the back of his head.

"Shut the fuck up. My mama wouldn't go for yo bum ass. You can barely pull a junkie." Bear pulled eggs, pork bacon, biscuits, and pork sausage out of the fridge. "You should be happy I came to wake your lazy ass up. You know you wasn't gon eat unless someone came to cook for you. Since Jakeshia left yo ass, you looking sad as fuck." Bear nudged Raoul on the shoulder and chuckled.

"Boy, fuck you. Her leaving me ain't stopped shit! And believe me, she'll be back once she starts missing this king ding-a-ling." Raoul grabbed his crotch through his pants.

"Boy, I heard you got that pack. She probably left yo ass after a doctor told her you gave her a sexually transmitted disease." Bear placed the biscuits in the oven and started cooking the bacon and sausage on the stove.

"I ain't gave nobody no damn STD. This dick here is clean. I told you, you betta ask ya mammy about me." Raoul went to the living room to roll up a blunt of weed.

"Aight now, keep talking that shit, you gon get yo ass folded up in yo own house. That foul ass mouth of yours ain't gone keep no female around. Just watch, you gone be old and lonely wishing you had treated at least one of these women better." Bear was engaged to his high school sweetheart. He always had his foot on Raoul's neck about respecting women. He knew Jakeshia was one of those women that you would only come across once in your lifetime. He always told Raoul to stop playing around with Amber and the many other females, but he was too hardheaded to listen.

"Aww, here yo ass go preaching again. I can't help it if the ladies love smooth ass Raoul. Why should I just have one when there's ten of them who will gladly get on their knees for me? Just because you stuck on one person doesn't mean I want the same." Raoul lit his blunt and started to smoke.

"You just don't get it, do you? Life isn't conquering all the women who want you. You creating all of these soul ties with women and don't even realize that these soul ties are the reason you have to stay drugged up and escape reality. Bruh, what do any of those females really do for you? Just think about it." Bear was finished cooking the meat and used the same skillet to start cooking the eggs.

"Boy, Amber got that stupid head, Madeline lets me hit that pussy however I like, and Nesha always bringing me over some bomb ass food. Shit, I'm over here living like a true king, my nigga." Raoul kicked his feet up and placed his hands behind his head.

"Yeah, you got problems my dude. Do you know all that shit you named could be found in one woman, ONE WOMAN! See, you lack the real skills, finesse, and work ethic to dedicate your efforts to finding that one. My fiancée brings everything I need to the table, and on top of that I don't have to worry about getting STDs and shit. She is my listening ear when I need to vent. She's my doctor when I'm feeling sick, all the meals she cooks are perfectly how I like them, when I'm ready to hit the road, I even have a companion to travel with. Everything you named is so mediocre bruh, and none of that shit is solid and guaranteed at the end of the day. Them females are not going to always be available once they find someone who treats them better." Bear shook his head at his friend's obvious ignorance and arrogance.

"Guess what Bear? When one ain't available, I got 20 mo lined up on go and ready." Raoul raised his phone in the air and pointed to his contacts.

"Well, where they at right now? You were sleep past 10 a.m. on a weekday, would rather starve all day instead of cooking your own food, your place looks like the Tasmanian Devil came through and wreaked havoc on every fucking thing. Like dude, this place is fucking filthy. You can't take better care of yourself and your place because you lack value and substance. Be honest with me, man. How are you really feeling?" Bear turned around to look at his friend.

"What Tony the tiger say? You're GRRREAT! Nigga, I'm good.

Life don't get no better than this shit right here." Raoul smiled, but deep down he felt some type of way about the question that Bear asked. Was he really good? Or was he putting on a front? Bear was done cooking everything and fixed both of them a plate. They chatted a little bit about sports until Bear had to leave to go work as security. Bear may not have utilized his size and talents to go into the NFL, but once the street life got old and too dangerous, he decided to make some legitimate money.

"Aight bro, thanks for cooking breakfast with MY groceries." Raoul laughed and went back to thinking about Bear's question. He couldn't help but think that Bear just might be on to something, but Raoul would never admit it. He went into a daydream about his first toxic experience with a female.

"Hey buddy, remember this will just be our little secret, okay?" Raoul's babysitter whispered to him as she patted him on the top of his head. He was ten years old and did not feel right about her touching him, but he knew how to keep a secret. He went to the bathroom and looked down at his private part to see if it had changed. Nope, still was the same. Lola had pulled and tugged at his private part, and he thought she may have made it stretchy like bubblegum. He couldn't understand why she would pull on his penis and make it go from soft and gushy to a straight, forward position. Was this a game that some teenagers played with kids? If so, he didn't like it.

But his mommy always told him to do what Lola told him to do. If Lola said keep a secret, he had to keep a secret. He left the bathroom and went to the living room to watch television. One of his favorite shows, Arthur, was on. He liked that Arthur had two parents at home, sisters, grandparents, good friends, and great teachers. Arthur and his friends were always doing different activities around their city. He wished that he could have his dad live in the house with his mom, maybe then his mom wouldn't have to work so much.

He hated being babysat by Ms. Lola. One day her niece came over, and she made them kiss. Another day she made her niece sit on top of Raoul's private area with their clothes on. Lola was very nice when his mom was around, but sometimes she yelled at Raoul when he didn't want to do what she asked. He wished he was Arthur. He sat in front of the TV laughing at D.W. and Arthur arguing over who was going to hold their baby sister Kate.

"Raoul, SHUT UP, you turd! I'm trying to paint my nails, and you're making me mess up!" Lola yelled as she stormed into the bathroom to grab a piece of tissue.

"I'm sorry, Ms. Lola." Raoul's eyes began to water. He didn't want to get hit for doing the wrong thing. He continued to watch the show until he fell asleep on the floor. The next morning, he was woken by his mom walking through the front door. He was so happy to see his mom.

"Mommy!" Raoul ran to his mom and jumped into her arms.

"Hey baby! How was your night? Did you have fun with Ms. Lola?" Raoul scanned the room, trying to avoid eye contact with Lola.

"Yes. Ms. Martha! We had a ball playing hide and seek, watching Arthur, and reading books. I guess I'll go home now. I had fun with you Raoul. See you next time." Lola grabbed her belongings and headed out the door. She was fifteen and lived a few doors down.

"What would you like for breakfast, baby?" Ms. Martha put her purse and jacket down on the couch and went into the kitchen to wash her hands.

"Can you make me some smiley face pancakes? They always cheer me up." Raoul loved pancakes, especially when his mom made them from scratch.

"Cheer you up? What happened baby, why do you need to be cheered up?" Ms. Martha stopped what she was doing to look at Raoul.

"Well, I accidentally made Ms. Lola upset because I made her mess up on her nail polish. But I didn't mean to." He fumbled with his fingers while looking at the floor.

"It's okay baby, she may have gotten a little upset, but it was something she was able to fix." She turned back around and started preparing the pancakes and other breakfast items. Ms. Martha was a single mother, but she made things happen for her son. She worked mornings most days, but occasionally she worked a double and needed Lola to watch Raoul on the weekends. In her eyes, Lola was heaven-sent. She was a very mature teenager who only charged her $15 to keep Raoul each time. That was the cheapest babysitter she was going to find. Sometimes she could find a family member that was available to watch him for free, but it seemed like some of her favors were running out. She finished breakfast and went to her room to go to sleep.

While she was asleep, Raoul was in his room playing with his private area. He started to mimic the same movements that Ms. Lola did to him. Her voice echoed in his head, "This will just be our little secret."

Raoul snapped out of the daydream to proceed with his day. While he was taking a shower, he immediately drifted into thinking about the first time that he and Jakeshia took a shower together. They got caught in the rain outside, so they were soaking wet. She suggested they take a shower and put on dry clothes, and Raoul agreed. While they were in the shower, he washed her back while she washed his. When he went to wash her vagina, he started to play with her clitoris as he slid two fingers inside of her. She exhaled in total bliss as he began to arouse her.

After a few minutes of pleasuring Jakeshia, he spun her around so she could face the wall. He gently inserted his penis inside of her and grabbed hold of her breast. He stroked her in slow motion while kissing her back and caressing her breast. They both moaned and began to grind faster.

"Dammit!" Raoul stopped himself from thinking about that night. He had gotten himself horny in the shower by himself and couldn't call Jakeshia or Amber to come help him with his issue. He finished showering and went to get dressed. Once he was dressed, he left his place to go meet up with the plug. At the time, Raoul was driving a 1995 Toyota Camry. He loved his car. It was reliable and good on gas. All the ladies loved riding with him because he kept it clean. In his eyes, all Toyotas and Hondas were classic and dependable cars.

He pulled up to the plugs spot and purchased two pounds of weed. Raoul had to hustle hard the next few days to pay his rent. He made a good amount of money but didn't know the first thing about budgeting. Jakeshia used to fuss at him all the time about the money he would blow in the club. He literally spent every dime he had, because he knew it wouldn't take much to run his money back up. Raoul never thought about the future, he was only living in the moment and surviving. Now that he had his product, he called one of his homeboys to see if they wanted to purchase anything from him. Raoul would get all types of drugs for super cheap and was able to sell them for double, sometimes triple his cost.

"Yoooo Slim! What it do, my boy?" Raoul rocked with Slim hard on the drugs. He knew he could trust Slim and didn't have to worry about no snake shit.

"Ruuuuueee! I can't call it mane. Just kicking it at the crib. Tell me you got some good news." Slim was the only one who called Raoul that.

"I do, I do, I do! It's looking like $800 for a pound my boy." Raoul's plug was the truth. Raoul was able to get two pounds of weed for $600. His trap was always bunkin'.

"Pull up on me ASAP! I need that, shit too dry this way! Let me get two from you!" Just like that, Raoul had bought and sold all of his weed. Once he met up with Slim, he planned on circling back to the plug to get three more pounds.

Raoul finished trappin' around 7 p.m. and went home bored. He didn't have any females to call and wasn't kissing anyone's ass. He eventually went to sleep early that night and had the worst sleep of his life. While he was asleep, he dreamed about his childhood when he was twelve years old. Lola was still babysitting him for his mom, and she was by then seventeen. By that time, he knew what she was doing when she would play with his penis. He had seen pornography movies where the woman would jack off the man's penis. Over the years, Lola had continued to sexually assault him, but she had stopped watching her niece.

Apparently, her niece had worked up the courage and threatened to tell her parents if Lola didn't stop messing with her. By the time Raoul was twelve, Lola was sucking his penis and had started to kiss him. Raoul was used to it now and no longer felt uncomfortable. This made him look at girls and women all the time, and he wanted to play with himself. One day while being babysat, Lola gave Raoul some wine.

"Raoul, let's take this wine with us into your bedroom." They walked back to his room, and she started to undress him. She was kissing him on his cheek and went to his lips. At first, he didn't kiss her back, but she fussed at him to kiss her. They began to kiss, and she told him to lay on his bed. She took his pants off and climbed on top of him. This was different for Raoul, but he didn't complain. He was starting to like Lola now that he was a little older. He was surprised at how good it felt. This was his first time, and with a girl who was five years older than him who'd been sexually assaulting him for 2 years. Raoul knew it was wrong since he never gave Lola permission, but at that moment it felt right.

The sex continued for a few months until Lola finally got her first real boyfriend. She continued to watch Raoul, but sometimes her boyfriend came over. The days that her boyfriend didn't come over, Raoul would try to initiate sex. He was hooked, but Lola always turned him down. One day Raoul threatened to tell his mom and Lola's boyfriend that she had been touching him. Out of fear, Lola gave in and started back having sex with him. About a year later, Lola had gotten pregnant.

"Raoul, I don't know what to do. I'm eighteen and pregnant, and I don't know if you're the dad or Steven." Lola cried out and laid on his bed.

"I don't know what you want me to do. I'm just a kid. You started all of this, so you need to figure it out. I'm just thirteen, so it's probably Steven's baby." Raoul shrugged his shoulders nonchalantly. "You can leave now. There's no use of me having sex with you now. Soon you'll be fat and ugly." Lola looked at Raoul in disgust. It was that day that Raoul knew that he could get what he wanted from females and throw them away when they no longer served him a purpose.

Raoul woke up out of his sleep around 4 a.m. to go grab a drink of water. He wondered what had ever happened to Lola. Once her parents found out she was pregnant, they sent her to the Midwest to go live with family. It was crazy to think that he may have a child out in the world that he'd never met. To that day he had never told anyone about how being sexually assaulted by his babysitter led to him having a sexual relationship with her. Raoul chuckled to himself as he thought about how he had been the man since he was a little boy. The women wanted him then, and they damn sure wanted him now. Well, all except Jakeshia. He had been calling and texting her for days now with no response. He looked at the clock and thought about calling her once he knew she would be up, but he decided that he'd reached out enough. "Raoul doesn't chase them, I replace them."

The next few days Raoul started feeling sick. He didn't have a cold or any flu-like symptoms, he just felt sick to his stomach and had the worst migraine. The self-medicated with Tylenol, that didn't help. He drank ginger and mint tea, but that didn't work. He ate tons of fruits, vegetables, and lean meats, but nothing helped. He couldn't figure out what was wrong. He refused to go to the doctor, because being nauseous and having a headache didn't sound severe to him. He called Bear to ask what he should do, so Bear brought over some chicken noodle soup and sat it at the front door. Raoul ate the soup and still felt nauseous.

Soon after, he dozed off for a nap and had a dream about Jakeshia leaving him. He started to cry in his sleep, realizing how much he actually missed her. What started out as a nap turned into a 12-hour deep sleep. When he woke up the next morning, it dawned on him that he was sick to his stomach because Jakeshia was missing from his life. He never acknowledged how much he loved her. He never acknowledged how his childhood assault led to him being a misogynist. As much as he loved women and having sex with them, deep down he hated their very existence. He hated that he had been taken advantage of at a young age. Although Lola was not much older than him. At the age of ten he was not ready for anyone to touch on him, he was not ready to be forced to lose his virginity at twelve, hell he definitely wasn't ready to become a father. All of those emotions hit Raoul, and he realized that he was fucked up in the head. He had held this secret for over a decade. He needed Jakeshia, he was ready to open up about his past. Jakeshia was the only one who he trusted enough and loved enough to help him deal with those scars.

It was past 8 a.m., so he decided to give her a call. He called her, left voicemails, sent text messages and still no response. He was going crazy! She was ignoring him in his time of need. She said she loved him, why would she ever leave? He left another voicemail. "Jakeshia! Please answer the phone! I need you! I miss you! I'm going crazy over here without you! I've been sick for a few days because you're not here. Please call me back. JAKESHIA! I can't live without you in my life!" Raoul hung up the phone and started crying. He decided to call her one more time. This time she answered, but he was not greeted with a pleasant voice. Jakeshia was at work and very irritated by his multiple attempts to get in touch with her. She told him to leave her alone and that she was done with him. That broke Raoul down even more.

At that moment Raoul felt worthless and didn't want to live anymore. Like many men, he had suppressed most of his emotions his whole life. Everything was hitting him at one time like a ton of bricks. He picked up his phone to call his mom. "Hey baby, I'm so glad you called me. I've been thinking about you. When are you going to come over so I can cook you a good meal?" Ms. Martha loved cooking for her only child.

"Mama, I won't be making it over to your house. I was just calling to tell you that I love you and I'll see you in heaven." After those words escaped his mouth, Raoul immediately hung up the phone. He grabbed his Taurus .38 handgun, placed the muzzle of the gun against the right side of his temple, shed his last tear, and squeezed the trigger. *CLICK, BOOM!*

Seven

Chapter 7

Jakeshia got off work on time and felt totally distraught. Raoul was in the hospital in critical condition and there was nothing she could do about it. She cried the entire ride to the house. She had never called Teresa or Mya back, but she knew exactly why they called her. When she arrived at the house, both of their cars were there. As soon as she walked through the door, she was bombarded with hugs from the both of them. They all cried together for a few minutes, and no one spoke. When they finally calmed down, Teresa handed Jakeshia a cup of ginger mixed with chamomile tea. "Here you go, girl. I knew you would need something to calm you down. I just can't believe this has happened. I just don't understand why he would do that." Teresa shook her head in disbelief.

"I don't understand it either. He was one of the hardest dudes we knew. He never came off as suicidal. How are they even sure that he did that?" Mya chimed in in disbelief.

"Y'all, he had been calling me all morning. Matter of fact, he had been calling, texting, and leaving voicemails for the past few days. In one of the voicemails today he threatened to kill himself, but I thought he was just talking crazy to get my attention. I had been ignoring him up until today. I finally got irritated and answered the phone. I told him to stop calling and that I was done with him for good. If I knew he was serious about taking his life, I promise I would've stayed on the phone to talk to him. He's always been emotionless. I just don't get it y'all, why would he do this? There were no signs leading up to this." Jakeshia shed a few tears as she drank her tea.

"Honestly Keshia, there was nothing you could have really done. I know you tried to give him all the love you possibly could. He didn't want it. He just wanted to play games with you, Amber, and all these other females. Had he ever been open to you about his feelings?" Teresa questioned Jakeshia.

"No. I always tried to get him to open up. Even when I expressed to him how I felt about him, he was nonchalant. Out of the seven years that we've been friends and have dated, he's only told me he loved me once. And the one time he said it, he was drunk off his ass. He never had deep conversations with me about his past, his dad, mom, or mood. We always talked about the here and now, drugs, sports, just basic stuff. I'm hoping he pulls through. His mom called me while I was at work, and she sounded like a wreck. She left the hospital because she couldn't handle it. You know he's her only child." They just sat there in silence until they all eventually fell asleep in the living room.

Jakeshia woke up the next morning with a missed call and text from Michael. Originally, she was scheduled to go into work, but she let her manager know that she had a family emergency to attend to. She decided to give Michael a call back and hoped that talking to him would take her mind off everything with Raoul. "Hey beautiful, glad you managed to call me this morning. I know you worked yesterday, so I figured you were tired when you got in." Michael was always understanding. They had been talking for close to a month now, and he was still consistent and the same as day one.

"Good morning. I actually received terrible news that my ex shot himself yesterday morning. So of course I was totally out of it." By now Jakeshia was drained and tired of crying. She was hoping for the best and wanted to refrain from crying.

"Oh my, I'm so sorry to hear that. I understand if you need time to process everything and need to talk some other time—"

Jakeshia cut Michael off, "No, I'm okay. He's at Grady in critical condition. But I'm going to keep pushing forward and hope for the best outcome. Do you want to go grab some breakfast?" Jakeshia asked Michael, hoping he was available.

"Absolutely. What do you have a taste for?" She could hear him moving around getting dressed.

"I was thinking we could go to this small spot near me named Mami's Kitchen." Jakeshia loved just about everything there, plus they were very inexpensive, so she ate there often.

"That works for me, love. I can pick you up if you'd like." Michael hadn't been to Jakeshia's yet and had respectfully never asked. With everything she was going through, he felt like it would be a good idea to offer to pick her up.

"I'd really like that. Today is one of those days that I don't feel like doing much, but I need to get out of this house so I don't drive myself crazy." Jakeshia gave Michael her address and promised to be ready in an hour.

An hour later, Michael arrived at Jakeshia's place and rang the doorbell. He was the first male she dated besides Raoul to ever come to her house, and Raoul never rang the doorbell. He always honked the horn or called her when he was outside. This was different to a man actually ringing the doorbell. It was kind of old school and she liked it. Jakeshia opened the door to invite Michael in to give him a tour of the house and to let her girls officially meet him. They walked around, and he gave the home's decor, size, and cleanliness multiple compliments. They stopped in the kitchen to talk to the girls.

"Good morning y'all. This is my good friend Michael. Michael, this is Teresa and Mya." Jakeshia pointed to each of her friends.

"It's nice to finally meet you two beautiful ladies. Jakeshia has told me a lot about y'all." Michael leaned in to give each of them a hug. He was such a southern gentleman. The girls were flattered by the compliment and the warm hug.

"Thank you, Michael. It's nice to meet you as well." Teresa and Mya almost sounded identical.

"Alright y'all, Michael and I are heading to Mami's Kitchen to grab breakfast. I'll see y'all later." Jakeshia walked out the front door as Michael led the way. He held her hand the entire way down the steps and opened the car door for her. "Thank you. You're such a gentleman." Jakeshia was smitten. Michael didn't cease to amaze her. Even his treatment towards her friends was spot on. She'd never dealt with a guy who was so comfortable and sweet when interacting with her friends. What had she really been settling for all these years? A guy who she'd known all of a month came in and treated her better than all of her exes put together.

"Listen, I appreciate you showing gratitude when I do things, but opening doors is the bare minimum. You don't have to thank me for doing things that should come naturally for a man." Michael knew she wasn't accustomed to a real man. Every chance she got she thanked him. He felt a little bad that such a beautiful and deserving woman had been treated poorly in the past.

"Michael, I'm always going to show appreciation for the things that you do. You don't have to do a lot of these things, but you choose to. And I love that about you." Jakeshia grabbed his hand and looked him in the eyes. At that moment, she forgot all about Raoul and his situation.

"Alright boo, if you say so. Just know I'll always choose to treat you like a lady." Michael leaned in and gave her a kiss on the cheek. They rode through Lithonia as Jakeshia talked about her childhood.

"I remember being about eight or nine years old walking to that neighborhood convenience store, at that time it was called Ja-Way Supermarket. We would always be at my aunt's house around the corner just hanging with my cousins. It's so crazy how time passes by, and I honestly haven't seen that side of my family in close to a decade. There wasn't a falling out or anything, I guess everyone just naturally grew apart once the elders got older or passed away." After a ten-minute ride, they made it to Mami's Kitchen.

"So what are you going to order? I'm thinking about getting the breakfast platter with salmon croquettes." Jakeshia loved her some salmon, and the biscuits at Mami's were homemade buttermilk biscuits that tasted like someone's grandma was in the back.

"That sounds delicious! I'm going to get the tenderloin biscuit with a side of hash browns and grits." A few moments later, they were at the front of the line to order. They both stuck with their initial meal ideas and ordered tea as their beverages. They sat down at an open booth for two and began to dig in.

"So, what do you think?" Jakeshia asked before she took a sip of her tea.

"This food is bomb. This biscuit… why didn't you tell me to order two? This is slap ya grandma good! I'm going to order food to go for sure. I really get the down south home feeling from this place. They are busy, but the service is fast and accommodates the line." Michael was halfway done with his food and hadn't even touched his tea.

"I mean I love the food here, but I wanted you to generate your own opinion of the food. Some people don't like southern cuisine like this." Jakeshia continued to finish off her food.

"Yeah, I understand. This place is small and appears to be in a random standalone spot, but these usually are the best type of restaurants. You can tell everything is fresh and cooked in house daily. Those big chain restaurants usually have a lot of pre-made items. We can eat here every day of the week if you like." They both giggled. They chatted a little while longer until they decided to head back to Jakeshia's around noon. They got back to Jakeshia's house, and she invited Michael in. They went to the living room to watch a little TV. A rerun episode of Maury was on, so they decided to watch a little messy TV. Jakeshia rested her head on his shoulder and soon drifted away for a nap.

Michael and Jakeshia woke up about two hours later to Jakeshia's phone ringing. She looked around startled, searching for her phone. She found it in her purse on the counter and saw that it was Ms. Martha calling. She managed to answer the phone before it hung up. "Hello." Her voice was raspy from being asleep.

"Hey Jakeshia. I was just calling to give you an update on

Raoul." She had forgotten all about Raoul from the great breakfast she had with Michael.

"Oh yes, how is he doing?" Now she had a knot in her stomach out of fear of the news.

"So the doctors were able to stabilize him yesterday and remove most of the fragments of the bullet. Due to all the stress on his body, the doctor placed him in a coma and wants to keep him in one as they monitor his condition." Ms. Martha sounded very hopeful, like a totally different person from the previous day.

"That sounds like great news. I'm hoping everything works out. Thank you for keeping me updated. Please let me know if anything changes, and let me know if you need anything." Jakeshia let out a loud sigh and stood there for a second. She wanted to collect herself before she went over to Michael. She walked back to the couch, laid her head on Michael's lap, and closed her eyes.

"Everything okay sweetheart?" Michael asked as he started to rub Jakeshia's head.

"That was my ex's mom. She said they removed most of the bullet from his skull and placed him in a coma. She sounded hopeful, so I'm guessing everything will be alright." She kept her eyes closed to keep from crying. She didn't want Michael to see her upset, and she didn't want to be upset about Raoul while spending time with Michael.

"That's good that he's still holding on. Is there anything I can do to cheer you up? Let me give you a foot massage." Michael was playing with fire. Acts of service was one of Jakeshia's love languages. She absolutely loved receiving massages. When Raoul would give her a massage, it only lasted 5 minutes then boom, sex.

"I would appreciate that. My feet are still aching from work yesterday." Michael and Jakeshia rearranged themselves on the couch so that her head was laying on the arm while her feet rested in Michael's lap. He started to massage her left foot gently, and she immediately felt a sense of relief. It had been a while since anyone had catered to her in this manner. Men were always so quick to get you in the bed but rarely satisfied other physical needs. She loved giving Raoul massages, just because she knew it relieved tension. Michael massaged both of her feet for a good twenty minutes, then asked if she wanted a back massage. She excitedly agreed and said that she would go to change her shirt. She changed into a tank top so that he could have better access to the entire surface of her back and brought a bottle of peppermint oil with her.

"I think this oil will help out with the massage." He went to the kitchen to grab a chair to place next to the couch. She laid on her stomach and turned to face the TV. Maury had gone off some time ago, so now Jerry Springer was playing. As he massaged her back, she couldn't help but to close her eyes. The massage felt so good, and she started to think about all the other things that he could manage to do with that muscular chocolate body of his. She stopped herself from thinking too much because she didn't want to get anything started. Four weeks wasn't nearly enough time for her to get physical with Michael.

She was determined to take things slow just to be sure that he was the right guy to get into her next relationship with. She wasn't playing any games, and he didn't seem to be playing any either. She thought to herself, *what could it truly hurt if we get physical?* After all, it had pretty much been a month, and he'd been the most consistent person she'd ever met. She told herself that if Michael made any sexual advances, she would go along with them.

"How are you feeling?" Michael asked as he applied some of the peppermint oil and started to massage her lower back.

"This feels amazing. Did you go to school to be a massage therapist?" Jakeshia asked while tilting her head to the side.

"Naw, I guess you can say I have a way with my hands." Michael chuckled, and for once sounded slightly vain. But as humble as he is, it definitely came off as confidence opposed to arrogance.

"You definitely do. You have me so relaxed that you're going to put me to sleep." Jakeshia wanted him to lay her body down and put her to sleep in a different way though.

"Damn, it feels that good? I'm flattered." Michael made his way back up to Jakeshia's shoulder and started applying more pressure. She moaned out loud as he massaged out a knot.

"You're pretty tense. When I'm done you need to make sure you drink a lot of water so that you can flush your body of these toxins." He massaged her for another ten minutes or so then went to go fix her some water. He was making himself at home, even though this was his first over. Jakeshia actually liked his comfortability. They had had the best conversations on the phone, their food dates were always fun and enlightening, and his energy was positive.

"Thank you. Let's chill some more and watch some movies." Jakeshia enjoyed his company. She started clicking through the channels and found 'Love and Basketball'. That was the perfect movie for them to watch.

So much time had elapsed that they had managed to watch three other movies. Jakeshia had ordered pizza and wings for their lunch so they could relax longer. It was now 9 p.m., and they were getting tired. "I guess I should be heading out." Michael stood up and looked down at Jakeshia. She didn't know what to say, but she surely didn't want to be alone. They just looked at each other. "Are you okay?" Michael asked.

Jakeshia was hesitant to speak. "I don't want you to leave yet… Do you mind staying over tonight?" He felt like home, and she didn't want the night to end.

"Of course I can stay. I can sense that you still don't feel too well from all the bad news." Michael sat back down next to her and gave her a hug. He was so warm and still smelled like his cologne.

"I guess we could go get comfortable in my room, I am getting a little tired." They walked back to her room, and she showed him around. In her tour earlier she pointed to her bedroom but didn't bother to show him everything.

"This is nice. You have it looking like a queen's palace." Michael was referring to the king-sized bed with all the decorative pillows.

"Thank you. It's just me, but I love a huge bed. Plus, sometimes I let my niece and younger cousins come spend the night." She went into the bathroom to change into her pajamas. Normally she would shower before getting into her bed, but she figured she would wash her bedding the next day since Michael was probably going to climb in without a shower. She made her way back into her bedroom with a short and tank top pajama set on, nothing too sexy. She was very cautious with her attire, as she didn't want Michael to think she was trying to dress naked to arouse him. She cozied up in the bed and told Michael he could lay in the bed or anywhere in the room, if he liked.

"I don't want to invade your space. I can lay on the floor; do you have an extra blanket?" Either Michael was being a complete gentleman, or something was really wrong with him. Would he really pass up the opportunity to lay next to Jakeshia for the first time? Did she stink or something?

"I actually don't have any extras. I left them at my cousin's house one day when we had a screen on the green. But if you're not comfortable here, I'll be okay by myself for the night." At that point, Jakeshia didn't want to seem desperate for company. She was giving Michael a way out.

"Oh naw, I'm cool with staying here. I just don't have any night clothes, and I remember what you said about outside clothes in your bed." Michael was actually being considerate.

"I understand. You're fine. You can just sleep how you are." Michael got in the bed but left plenty of space between him and Jakeshia. She turned the TV on and turned her bedroom light off. About five minutes later, she made her way into Michael's arms and fell asleep.

The next morning, Jakeshia woke up but didn't make a move. She was still in Michael's warm arms. She was surprised that he hadn't tried anything with her. No fondling, no kissing, no nothing. Again, she didn't know whether to take it as an insult or to compliment Michael. After laying in silence thinking to herself for a few minutes, she finally turned her TV on to catch the news. A bunch of accidents, traffic, killings, and robberies appeared on the screen. She hated watching the news, it was always sad. Soon after she turned on the TV, Michael woke up.

"Good morning beautiful." He gave her a kiss on the cheek.

"Good morning." She didn't turn her head since she was embarrassed by her morning breath, but there was a cure for that. She immediately went to the bathroom to brush and floss her teeth. When she came out, she brought an unopened spider man toothbrush for Michael.

"Well, this is the only unused toothbrush I have that isn't pink with unicorns." They both laughed in unison.

"Thank you, this will do just fine." Michael went to the bathroom to pee and brush his teeth. When he came out, Jakeshia was sitting at the edge of her bed staring at him. He stopped and stared for a moment too. He was stuck and didn't know what to say. He looked at her in amazement. "You're even stunning when you first wake up in the morning." He slowly walked over to her and gave her a gentle kiss on her lips as he caressed the nape of her neck. *DAMN!* was all Jakeshia could think. Michael pulled her pajama pants down, softly pushed her shoulders down for her to lay on the bed, then rhythmically started to lick and kiss on her vagina. His lips were so soft and pleasant. He knew exactly what he was doing, and Jakeshia couldn't help but to moan out loud in ecstasy. She grabbed the back of his head, and that made him get even more intense with his tongue game. He had a pattern in motion going from her clitoris back to her vagina.

A few seconds later she orgasmed. "Oh my god! That was out of this world!" Jakeshia couldn't move, she was stuck laying there motionless.

"You tasted so good." Michael went to the bathroom to grab a washcloth to wash Jakeshia off. That was it, he simply wanted to please her with nothing in return. When he walked back, she could see that he had an erection, but she could tell that Michael was okay with not having sex at the moment. After he wiped her down, he laid next to her and pulled her closer to cuddle. She could feel his erection through his pants. She started to rub on his penis and noticed that he had a good length to it, which made her smile on the inside. She was happy that he was working with something. Most women liked a man with a big 'third leg'.

She continued to rub on his penis, and they began to kiss. Michael grabbed her butt and squeezed it. He was such a great kisser. She attempted to unfasten his pants, but he stopped her. All she could think was, *what the fuck?* "Today was all about pleasing you. I know he's excited, but I can take a backseat today." Michael moved her hair out of her face and gave her a peck on the lips. Jakeshia liked the fact that he only wanted to please her, but at this point she wanted a piece of him. If his dick game was anything like his tongue game, she would be satisfied every time.

"Damn, I guess I can respect that. I've never been turned down though." She still felt some type of way. "Oh naw, queen, this isn't me turning you down from anything. I simply wanted to please you and hope to raise your spirits. I don't think this is the right time for me to have sex with you based on what you're currently going through. I want to make sure that our first time is something special. I would feel like I was taking advantage of your vulnerability right now. Don't feel like anything is wrong with you, I promise you're just perfect in my eyes." Damn, Michael had the gift of gab. He always knew what to say and how to say it. Sometimes it was hard to tell if this was all real, or if he just knew how to run a game on her.

"Okay… this has been a rough few days. So what do you have planned today?" Jakeshia wanted to change the subject. Sex was clearly off the table.

"I actually have an afternoon class to attend. I should be heading out sooner than later so I can clean up before school."

Michael sat up and stretched his arms. Jakeshia didn't want him to go, but she knew how the grind went. She wasn't in the mood for school, but she too had classes. Michael left, and she got herself together for her classes. She was determined to turn her mood around. Raoul was still in critical condition, but at least they had him stable. She left home for school and decided that she would do a little shopping and have some girl time later.

Eight

Michael's Story

"Ma, everything is going to be okay. Just get up." Five-year-old Michael was crying and pulling on his mother's arm as she laid bloody on the floor. His father had beat her up in one of his drunken rages. His dad was a construction worker by day and an alcoholic by night. Many nights he would come home from the bar and get upset at any and everything. This night in particular he wanted to eat steak and potatoes when he got home, but Olivia had cooked pork chops. As always, she had his plate ready in the microwave when he got home. When he opened the microwave to see pork chops, he threw the plate at the wall, and the glass shattered into pieces. Michael ran behind the kitchen table in fear to avoid getting struck across the face.

Immediately after the plate hit the wall, his dad went to slap Olivia. She fell to the floor and balled up into a fetal position. He started to punch her in the face and kick her in the side.

"You stupid BITCH! You can't never get anything right!" he barked at her and spit on her before he went to lay out on the couch. That was when Michael found it safe to go check on his mom. He hated his dad for beating on her. Olivia was the sweetest woman and didn't deserve the abuse.

When she stood up, she noticed that a lot of the blood on the floor was coming from her vagina. She was about three months pregnant with their second child. As she looked at the amount of blood on the floor and felt her belly cramping, she knew she was having another miscarriage. "Michael, go in your room and pack your suitcase and backpack full of clothes. We're leaving tonight." She looked over at the pathetic excuse of a man who was snoring on the couch and knew that he was out for the night. It was the perfect time to get away. Olivia was so tired. She had been getting abused for the past four years. She went to her room and gathered all the clothes that she could fit in her two suitcases. She went under her bed to retrieve the $5,000 she had managed to save up unnoticed and collected her photo albums. Once they were both packed up, they quietly got into the car and drove off.

The next day Michael woke up, and he was at his grandmother's house. His mom had driven five hours from Clarksville, Tennessee to Marietta, Georgia. Michael was so happy to see his grandma. "Heeeyyy grandma!" Michael squealed as he jumped up to give her a hug.

"Hey, baby. I see you finally got up." Grandma Mae had cooked breakfast, and Michael could smell the butter that was melted on her homemade biscuits. "Come on in here and fill up that belly, boy. I know you must be hungry." He hurried in the kitchen behind his grandma.

"Where's mommy?" Michael was worried. The last time he saw his mom, she was bruised and bloody.

"Oh, don't you worry about your mama. She's out with your uncle Robert right now. They'll be back a little later." Robert had taken his sister to the hospital to get checked out. When she arrived early that morning all bruised, he was furious. He was going to head to Tennessee with his 12-gauge shotgun, but Olivia convinced him that she needed him to take her to the hospital. Robert hated Michael's dad. In all these years, he had only seen his sister and nephew two or three times a year. They were isolated from their family and being controlled like possessions.

Robert was the younger brother, but he always protected his sister growing up. Before their dad passed away, he promised that he would take over as the man of the house, and he took his promises seriously. Michael ate all of his breakfast and asked to go outside to play, and his grandma willingly said yes.

While Michael was outside, the phone rang. "Hello." Grandma Mae had that pleasant southern charm about herself that radiated to the other end of the phone.

"Mae, where is your daughter and my son?" It was Michael's dad.

"Boy, when you call my house, you need to lower your voice. I don't know who raised you, but I assure you that yesterday was your last time touching my baby." Mae was a sweetheart but did not play about her kids.

"Ma'am, I am on my way to come get my son." He had lowered his voice, but she still did not like the way he was talking.

"You listen here, you no good excuse of a man. My child and this here grandson of mine will be staying with me from now on. You are not welcome here or anywhere near them. Yesterday was the last time. Now you can try to come this way if you'd like, but I promise that my son and I will have something waiting on you. Hear me loud and clear when I tell you, they are my flesh and blood, and I will put you six feet under before they ever go back to Tennessee to live with you. Now you carry on about your day, boy, and don't call my house anymore ya hear." Grandma Mae hung up the phone just as Olivia was entering the house.

"Hey baby. What did the doctor say? How's the baby?" Olivia broke out into tears and fell into her mother's arms.

"Mama, he beat the baby out of me." This was the second miscarriage that she had had due to domestic violence.

"Oh baby, everything is going to be alright. You're home with mama now. Let's go in the back to take a nice, warm sponge bath." The ladies walked to the back of the house as Robert went outside in a rage. Robert swore that he would kill that man if he ever laid eyes on him again.

By the time Michael was eight years old, his mom was married to his stepdad, Miles. After Miles and Olivia tied the knot, they moved into a beautiful colonial home in Decatur, Georgia. Michael was so excited to have a new home with a huge front and back yard. He had his own room with lots of toys, games, and books. He was able to eat dinner every night with his mom and Miles at the dinner table. For the first time in his life, he felt like he was at home with HIS family. Miles did not have any kids of his own but treated Michael as if he was his biological son. Michael loved Miles. He was kind, loving, supportive, generous, and very hands-on. He taught Michael everything about sports, and even helped him with his schoolwork.

For so long Michael wished that his dad would come around

to do things with him, but he hadn't seen him since the night they left Tennessee. He hadn't even spoken to him since then. It was like his dad had disappeared into thin air. While in Georgia, his Uncle Robert and Miles managed to fill the void of not having a father around, and they were doing a great job. By that time, his uncle Robert had married the love of his life and moved out of Grandma Mae's house. Everyone's life was falling into place and young Michael was loving it.

"Push baby, you can do it! She's almost out!" Miles was cheering Olivia on while she was in labor with their first and only baby girl. Moments later, Grace was out of her mother's womb and crying. "She's so beautiful. Hi, Grace. Welcome to the world." Olivia was so happy to welcome her first daughter. She wanted to give her daughter a name with meaning. After her two previous miscarriages, she was so thankful to have another child, and this time with a man who loved her and Michael. "We are so blessed to have you here with us Grace!" Miles shed a few tears. He had never experienced something so pure. Grace was perfection. Olivia placed Grace on her chest for skin to skin contact and moved her mouth toward her nipple so she could begin breastfeeding. Grace latched on immediately, which brought so much joy to her parents. She was adorable and greedy too. After the doctor checked Olivia one final time, Miles went to get Mae, Robert, and Michael. Michael was so excited to see his new baby sister. He was proud to be a big brother, and this enthusiasm would continue on in life. One year later, Michael would welcome his little brother into the world, and Liam would complete their family.

"Ma, can Grace and I go outside to play?" Michael loved being outside. He knew that if he offered to bring Grace, his mom would say yes every time. Although Michael was nine and Grace was one, they had a very strong bond. He helped out a lot with Grace and Liam, who was three months old at the time. "Yes, you two can go to the backyard. Check to make sure that the gate is closed and keep your sister safe. I'll be watching you from the kitchen window." Olivia was making lunch for her kids while Miles was out running errands. Grace was playing with her pink playground ball when a black and yellow snake got close to her. Michael saw the snake, picked up Grace and took her in the house. Instead of telling his mom what he had seen, he grabbed a shovel.

He walked back over to the snake, who hadn't moved, and hit it multiple times over the head. This was the first time that Michael had the ability to protect a loved one. He was traumatized from seeing his mom get abused and refused to allow the snake to hurt his family. Once he knew the snake was dead, he walked back into the house like nothing happened. Olivia asked him what he was doing with the shovel and why he had brought Grace back into the house. He explained his feelings about the snake without blinking an eye. At that moment, Olivia knew that her son may need counseling. He had seen his dad abuse his mom on multiple occasions, and it never dawned upon her that Michael may begin to project his fear and anger out into the world. Once Miles returned home, Olivia sat down with him to have a talk. They agreed to find a family therapist the next day. This was the first step of Michael's development into a healthy and healed young man.

When Michael went to high school, all of the girls wanted him. He was the classic tall, dark, and handsome jock. Although the girls threw themselves at him, he was too focused on track, basketball, baseball, and school work. His mom and Miles always taught him to be respectful to women. One day Olivia told him, "If you don't have interest in them, don't entertain them. I don't care what games your little friends are playing. My son will value and respect women and their time. Always imagine how you want Miles to treat me. I love you son." Those words always resonated with Michael. So since he wasn't interested in anyone, he never wasted anyone's time.

Besides, he was too fixated on being successful. His mother graduated high school but never went to college, he wanted to break that generational curse and be the first college graduate of their family. The standard was set so all he had to do was stay dedicated and put in the work. His senior year he had gotten accepted into many schools across the country including The Howard University. He was in limbo for a while trying to decide where he wanted to go to school. By the end of the fall semester, he decided to accept his full ride basketball scholarship to Morehouse College. Morehouse was a division two school at the time, and it was close to home. Michael was all about family and didn't want to be hours away from his family. He loved spending time with Grace and Liam, and being away for college would greatly impact their bond. He also loved his parents and their connection. There was nothing comparable to the life they all had built together.

Michael told his family about his decision, and they were proud of him either way. Olivia was actually a little disappointed that Michael didn't choose to go out of state for school. She wanted her son to experience a different environment outside of the one he had grown up in, but she fully supported him. During the spring semester of Michael's senior year, he decided that he was no longer interested in playing basketball for Morehouse. He didn't have the passion for sports anymore. He spoke with the recruiter, who didn't agree with his choice but understood. Throughout high school Michael had maintained a 3.9 grade point average. Thanks to his GPA, he was able to receive a full ride academic scholarship to Morehouse, which replaced the athletic scholarship. His focus throughout the years managed to pay off in a major way. Many of his classmates had failed classes, received low C's, and had to complete recovery courses to graduate on time. Michael was breaking generational curses within his family and paving the way for his younger siblings. He had wished that his biological dad could've been a part of his journey, but he failed to show up no matter how many invitations he mailed to their old address. Michael would later find out why his dad could not make any of his events.

Nine

Chapter 9

Jakeshia was scrambling around looking for her keys. Ms. Martha had given her a call to let her know that after three weeks Raoul had finally woken up from his coma. Her heart skipped a beat when Ms. Martha gave her the good news. She was so anxious and couldn't wait to go to Grady to see Raoul. She finally found her keys in her closet on the floor.

"How the hell did they get in here?" The night before she had thrown her jacket into the closet and must've dropped her keys. She rushed out the door and headed to the hospital. While she was driving, Michael gave her a call.

"Hi babe, what are you up to?" Two weeks ago, Michael had asked Jakeshia to be his girlfriend, so now they were official.

"Hey boo, I am on my way to the hospital to see Raoul. His mom said he's woken from his coma." Jakeshia was very open with Michael about everything that was going on with Raoul's condition. Michael loved the fact that she was an empath.

"Oh wow, that's good news. Well, call me later when you get a chance." Michael could tell by her voice that she was overly anxious.

"I will. Talk to you later." They hung up the phone as Jakeshia hit ninety miles an hour on the highway. She arrived at the hospital in record timing. As she rode the elevator to the trauma floor, she began to feel nauseous. She didn't really want to see Raoul in a hospital, but there she was. She got to his room, and Ms. Martha was at his bedside. She crept slowly towards them, and her eyes began to water. Seeing him in that bed like that truly broke her heart. Raoul was so tough and resilient in the streets. She couldn't believe that he tried to end his own life.

"Hey Keshia, baby!" Ms. Martha brought her in for a big, warm hug.

"Hey Ms. Martha. You look amazing." Ms. Martha had shed some pounds and was looking like a young girl. Jakeshia shifted her attention over to Raoul, who looked happy to see her.

"Hey Raoul." Her voice was a little shaky.

"Hey." He couldn't really speak at the moment.

"The doctors say that he will need to do a few weeks or so of speech therapy. The trauma to his brain and the amount of time that he was comatose has affected various functions. They are hopeful for a full recovery though, it may just take some time." Ms. Martha was always an optimist. Raoul and Jakeshia just stared at each other. She couldn't help but cry. He reached for her hand to hold it, which soothed her. She and Ms. Martha sat and talked to each other and Raoul for about two hours.

"It has been good seeing you Raoul. I'm really happy you pulled through, and I'm sorry I didn't listen to you that day." Jakeshia felt terrible and blamed herself for what happened. Truth was Raoul's mental health was not her responsibility, especially after the way he treated her for years. Raoul didn't tell anyone what he was emotionally going through. Bear was his closest friend, and even he didn't know that Raoul was secretly battling depression. Everyone missed the signs. No one realized that he was overcompensating by drinking, smoking, and having sex with multiple women. Raoul's womanizing behavior all stemmed from his childhood experiences that no one knew about.

Jakeshia made it home late that day. She had missed two of Michael's calls and was too emotionally exhausted to call him back. She needed to get herself ready for bed since she had a few classes in the morning. As she went to turn on the water for her shower, the phone rang. It was Ms. Martha. Jakeshia started to panic; she was hoping it wasn't bad news.

"HELLO!" Jakeshia yelled over her running water.

"Hey Jakeshia baby. This is Ms. Martha. I just wanted to call and thank you for coming to support my baby." Jakeshia let out a sigh of relief and placed her hand over her chest.

"You're welcome, Ms. Martha. I've known Raoul too long to not show up. We may not be together, but I will always have love for him." In her mind it was sad what they had become. She no longer saw a future with the guy she envisioned spending the rest of her life with.

"I'm glad to hear these words. I know you two aren't together, but I could see it in his eyes that he really loves and cares about you. As he recovers, can you have it in your heart to be here for him? It would mean the world to him and me." All Jakeshia could think was, *what the fuck*. Ms. Martha was asking for too damn much. Jakeshia had moved on to a new relationship. One that had meaning with a man who showed that he was invested in evolving with her. It sounded like Ms. Martha wanted Jakeshia to just throw her life away and run back to Raoul. This put her in such a difficult place.

"Ms. Martha, I love y'all, I really do. But I don't think I can do that. I have a boyfriend, and I want to move forward with my life. I'm sincerely disheartened by what happened to Raoul and everything that he is going through, but I can't continue to put myself in a position to keep saving him. My presence can't save him. I've been here for years and at times he was the anchor holding me down. I hope you understand my decision." Jakeshia felt bad. She knew Ms. Martha had good intentions, but she refused to agree. Raoul clearly needed some mental help.

"I guess I understand. But I feel like there is still love there. I don't think you would've showed up the way you did if there wasn't. Just think about it for me baby and get back to me when you get a chance. I'll still be calling to give you updates on his condition. Have a good night, precious." They got off the phone, and Jakeshia was left on an emotional roller coaster. She went ahead and took her shower. Once she got out, she crashed on the bed without putting on a single piece of clothing.

"Uggghhh." Jakeshia was awakened by the sound of her phone ringing. She felt like she had been hit by a box truck carrying tons of bricks. She rolled over to look at her phone to see who it was calling, and it was Michael. "Hey babe." She answered through a raspy voice.

"Good morning, beautiful. It sounds like you are still asleep." Michael faithfully called Jakeshia every morning, but most days she was up by the time he called.

"Good morning, babe. Yes, I was asleep, but I need to get up and get ready for school." She looked at the clock and saw it was close to 8:30 a.m. She needed to hustle so she wouldn't be too late for her first class.

"How did everything go at the hospital yesterday?" Jakeshia never called Michael back the previous day, but he knew she had gotten tied up with Raoul.

"It was okay. He was definitely awake and out of his coma. He can't talk right now, but they say he will need some time in speech therapy to relearn how to talk again. He also damaged a few nerves from…" She hesitated to finish her sentence as she thought about how Raoul looked with the bandage over his head.

"It's okay, we don't have to talk about it. I really just wanted to call as I do every day to check on you. I know you have to get ready, so just call me later when you get some time." They got off the phone so she could get her day started. Michael was so understanding, and Jakeshia felt like her life was about to become a big mess again. She had broken up with Raoul and thought she'd completely moved on but seeing him in that hospital brought back so many good memories. She was now stuck on what her next move should be. Ms. Martha wanted her to be involved in Raoul's healing process, meanwhile she had a whole boyfriend that she really adored. She got dressed then packed a few items to eat for breakfast and lunch. Once she got into her car, she called Ms. Martha.

"Hey Jakeshia baby. How are you doing this morning?" Ms. Martha was always so full of life and love.

"Good morning Ms. Martha. I'm doing okay. I just wanted to call and check to see how you were doing and how Raoul is doing today." Jakeshia was extremely nervous about the response she was going to receive.

"He is doing very well. Your name was the first word he uttered today. I think he really wants you to come back to see him." Jakeshia didn't know what to say or feel. She was happy that he managed to speak, but she was torn about going to see him.

"Wow! It's really great that he's talking a little now. I have a lot of classes today, so I don't know about going to the hospital today. I can try to make it another day when I have a lighter schedule." She wanted to choose her words wisely. She didn't want to disappoint Ms. Martha.

"That sounds good baby. I know you work and go to school. I will tell him that you asked about him. You have a great day, you hear." They hung up the phone and Jakeshia cried the remainder of her ride to school.

After a long day full of classes, Jakeshia just wanted to get home and take a bubble bath. On her ride home, she called Michael because she really missed him. It seemed like the last few days had been fully consumed with Raoul. "Hi baby, I really needed to hear your voice." She smiled when he picked up the phone.

"Hey beautiful. I'm glad you had time to call. I know these past few days have been hectic, so I understand. What are you up to?" She loved how consistent and understanding Michael was.

"I'm actually headed home, super exhausted." She had just gotten on the highway and landed in some traffic.

"Oh okay. What are you planning to eat for dinner? I could order you some delivery or bring something for you." The perfect gentleman.

"It's okay babe. I'm going to make myself a salad. I'm not in the mood to eat anything heavy. But enough about me, how has your day been?" It seemed like the past few days had been consumed with her and her baggage, and she really hadn't checked in on her man and his life. She just shook her head.

"Baby, I love hearing about you and your day. My day has been pretty good. I went by my parents' house to spend some time with Grace and Liam. I really missed them. It's crazy that I'm minutes away, but I just don't have the time to stop by there every day." Jakeshia could hear the minor sadness in Michael's voice as he expressed disappointment in himself. She knew that Michael was close with his family and absolutely adored his siblings. Unlike Michael, Jakeshia didn't have such a close-knit family.

"Aww, that's so good to hear. I know they loved seeing you. They didn't have school today?" Jakeshia was confused about how he managed to spend time with them during the middle of the school week.

"No school for them today. They were off and the teachers had a workday." Jakeshia loved when her teachers had a workday when she was younger. On those days she always walked to one of her friends' houses and hung out while everyone's parents were at work. They behaved themselves but it was always fun being able to hang without adult supervision. She remembered one time in tenth grade when she and her girls went to JD's crib with his rap group. They were the most poppin' rap group in their school. While at JD's, she was asked to hop on one of the records because they needed a female on the song. At first, she was nervous, but she secretly wrote verses in her spare time at home. Everyone was so surprised at how fire her verse was. From that day on, they started calling her Lady Keezy. She recorded two more songs with them but never pursued anything with music. It was all fun and games for Jakeshia.

"I used to love teacher workdays. How is Grace doing in ballet?" Jakeshia hadn't met any of Michael's family, but she remembered every single detail he'd ever shared about them.

"She is doing well. She got chosen to be the lead in the story ballet performance at her school." Michael always raved about how proud he was of Grace and her accomplishments. Grace was the rainbow baby and really did bring so much joy, light, and laughter into her family's life.

"That is wonderful. I'm already super proud of her and we haven't even met!" They were taking things slow, no need to rush, especially with her new baggage.

"My family keeps asking about the woman who has me smiling at my phone all the time. They are anxious to meet you." Michael wanted to set something up with his family and Jakeshia but respected Jakeshia's wishes to take it slow.

"Aww, I have you smiling a lot?" Jakeshia blushed.

"Girl, stop it, you know you have me making all kind of googly eyes." Michael chuckled.

"I know, I know. But babe I'm going to have to call you back, someone is calling my other line." Jakeshia clicked over, and it was Ms. Martha.

"Hey Jakeshia. I really need you to come to the hospital. I have something you need to see." Jakeshia shook her head and immediately got frustrated.

"Hey Ms. Martha, can it wait? I just got out of school and am heading home." She really didn't want to be bothered with Raoul's madness today.

"Honestly baby, it is really monumental. I don't think this can wait." Ms. Martha was really insisting that Jakeshia make her way to the hospital. Jakeshia sighed and agreed to go. She got off the next exit and turned around to head in the opposite direction.

Jakeshia reached the hospital in about fifteen minutes. Once she entered Raoul's room, she was surprised to see him up and slowly moving around using a walker. It was amazing that he was active, he hadn't been out of his coma a week yet. The doctors said it was a miracle. Apparently, he had gotten a sensation in his toes that morning, then he started moving his legs. Around lunch time, he told Ms. Martha that he wanted to try to walk. At first, she disagreed, but as stubborn as he was he placed his feet on the floor to show her he had some strength. The nurse was called in and decided to page the physical therapist on duty. Jakeshia walked in just in time to see him working with the physical therapist for the first time. Originally, he wasn't scheduled to meet with a PT until after he was discharged next week, but his insistence to walk definitely sped up the process.

"Wow Raoul…. you're doing a great job." Jakeshia spoke softly as tears of joy gathered in the corner of her eyes. "Hey Jakeshia." Raoul was able to whisper with a groggy voice. Although he was still regaining strength in his vocal cords, she fully understood his words. It was amazing how much he was progressing, and Jakeshia could no longer fight the tears. She just smiled at him with a warm feeling in her heart. Ms. Martha walked over to give her a hug. At that moment, they cried silently together. Raoul stopped in his tracks to stare at them.

"You have done a great job so far Raoul. Let's call it a day and do some more work tomorrow. It's important that we take things slowly as you rebuild your leg muscles." The physical therapist helped Raoul back to his bed and took the walker out of the room. "I'll see you tomorrow, tough guy." The physical therapist closed the door behind her.

"So how are you feeling today, Raoul?" Jakeshia asked as she stood near the door.

"Feeeeeling blessssssssed. Tha..nks for cccccooooming." Raoul was slurring his words, but he was doing a great job of speaking. He was definitely proof that miracles could happen and everyone's body recovered at its own pace. He was surpassing all of the assumptions made by his doctor's.

"You are truly blessed. I mean look at you, walking and talking. You were always the toughest guy I knew." Jakeshia chuckled. "There really isn't anything that can stop you, and I'm so happy that you are recovering at such a fast rate." Jakeshia smiled as she made eye contact with Raoul. At that moment, a wave of emotions hit her. She loved him, and she missed the good old days. Raoul had his moments where he was extremely sweet, but he just wasn't loyal to her. "It was so great to see you today, Raoul. I'm sorry I can't stay longer but I really need to get home to do schoolwork." She knew she needed to leave before she got sucked back into his trance. Seeing him be so vulnerable made her want to play superwoman. But deep down she knew that he could never be the man she desired or needed. She gave him a hug.

"I love you Jakeshia." Raoul whispered in her ear and gave her a kiss on the cheek. She didn't respond, just said her goodbyes and left. As she walked back to her car, she cried, thinking, *why does life have to be so fucking complicated?* If Raoul had treated her better or even been faithful, they'd still be together. He wouldn't be in the hospital and would've never shot himself. The reality was, Raoul had to deal with his own demons and reap his own karma. She was not going to fall prey to his womanizing behavior anymore.

Jakeshia made it home in about forty minutes. When she arrived, she was exhausted physically and mentally. Mya and Teresa were home chilling in the living room. "Hey y'all. It's good to finally see my girls." Jakeshia slammed her book bag on the floor and went straight to the refrigerator for some orange juice.

"Hey Keshia girl! So, what's good with Raoul? I know you've spoken to Ms. Martha." Mya asked her in concern.

"I actually just left from seeing him. Y'all, he is doing so well. It's only been six days since his incident and he is talking but slurring his words. Today Ms. Martha called me there so I could see him walking with a walker. They did not expect him to be doing any of these things so soon!" She was excited to share the good news.

"Damn, that man is a soldier for real." Teresa said.

"Yeah, he is. I don't think I can go back to see him. This whole thing is bringing back too many emotions that I thought I was over. When I went to leave, I gave him a hug and he told me he loved me. Do y'all know that he has probably only told me that less than five times." Jakeshia shook her head as she took another sip of her juice.

"Well, you always knew he loved you, he just had a hard time keeping his dick in his pants." Teresa chuckled as she was being brutally honest.

"I mean yeah, but I can't deal with dating anyone and not being reassured that I'm the only one. I have this great thing going on with Michael, and he is just so perfect. He's a family man, gentle with me, always wants to talk on the phone or see me, extremely ambitious and intelligent, he works so hard at his schoolwork. I mean, he really is the whole package, not to mention he is tall, dark and handsome." Jakeshia blushed and licked her lips. Thinking about Michael really excited her. She had history with Raoul, but he never made her feel like a lady the way Michael did.

"Yeah, Michael does seem to have it going on, girl. I hope Raoul recovers, but fuck having a relationship with him. He lost you and showed you who he is. Don't get sappy now and fuck up this good thing you got going on." Teresa was absolutely right. Cherish those memories, but fuck that tired ass relationship.

Ten

Teresa's Story

"Hey ma'am, how can I help you?" Teresa was working the cash register at her job. This was her fourth year working at Forever 21, and she was pretty burned out.

"I wanted to try these outfits on, but I see you have the fitting room closed. Could you be a doll and open one for me?" The older lady was sweet, but the sign clearly stated the fitting rooms were closed for maintenance.

"Well ma'am, our fitting rooms are closed today for maintenance." Teresa responded in a very professional tone.

"So I guess y'all don't want my hard earned money? It's a shame, a girl like you should be willing to help me out and provide the best service possible." Now the lady was striking a nerve.

"Excuse me? A girl like me? What does that mean? I'm a grown woman just like you, just younger." Teresa cocked her head to the side and tried her best to keep her tone appropriate.

But she didn't play the disrespect game with nobody!

"You're still a girl boo. But let me get out of this ghetto store before you and these other hoodlums try to steal my credit card information." The lady was totally out of pocket.

"BYE! Get out and don't come back! I don't know who you think you're talking to or talking about but bi—" One of Teresa's co-workers stopped her before she could finish cursing the woman out.

"Teresa!!! Girl, let that shit slide, we are at work! You know these folks are crazy, don't lose this job over that!" Her co-worker was right, but Teresa did not take kindly to the older woman's tone. Teresa decided to go to the break room to let off some steam. As she paced back and forth in the break room, she thought about all the times her mom and dad had spoken to her in a condescending tone. Her family was so toxic, so outside of their house she always felt like she had to fight anyone who thought they were going to disrespect her. There were plenty of days that she went to school with bruises and black eyes because her mom had beaten her.

"Get your ass back in here!" Teresa's mom yelled as she pulled her back in the house by her hair. She threw her to the ground and started kicking her in the back.

"Ma, stop it. Please! You're hurting me!" Fifteen-year-old Teresa cried out in pain.

"No, your lil hoe ass is going to learn to stay in a child's place! You don't tell me what you're not going to do up in here!" Teresa had told her mom that it wasn't her turn to wash the dishes. In fact, it wasn't, it was one of her younger siblings' turn, but her mom didn't care.

"I'm sorry! I'll go do the dishes! Pleeeaaase just stop hitting me!" Teresa was in pain, with a bloody nose, and winded. Her mom hit her two more times then stopped.

"Next time when I ask you to do something, you better not say shit to me! You understand?" It was obvious that her mom was high on drugs. She got hit often by her mom, but the beatings came when she had done cocaine.

"Yes ma'am. I understand you." Teresa got up and immediately went to wash the dishes. All of her siblings stayed in their rooms minding their business. It was crazy that she was the only one who got physically abused in the house. Her brother, Rico, who was a year younger than she was, could talk back with no consequences. Once she finished the dishes, she went into the bathroom to clean herself up. When she looked in the mirror, she burst out into tears. She looked so ugly. Her hair was mangled, blood gushing from a few cuts on her face, purple bruises on her face and torso, and her lip was swollen.

She was so sick and tired of how her parents treated her. She wanted to run away but didn't have any family that lived in Georgia. She ran bath water and placed Epsom salt in the tub. The Epsom salt would help ease the pain of her bruises. Once she finished bathing, she followed up with peroxide on all the areas that were bleeding. She didn't have any bandages, so she placed Vaseline over her open wounds hoping that none of them would get infected. Every time her mom beat her up, she was exhausted emotionally and physically, so she decided to go to bed early without eating.

Teresa snapped out of her daydream and was crying as she stood in the break room. She was so angry and had so much hurt built up. She really wanted to hurt someone. Her work shift was ending soon, so she decided that she would leave a few minutes early since her mood was fucked up. "Yo, I'm out. I'll see y'all people tomorrow." She threw the deuces at her co-workers and manager as she walked out of the store. With everything going on in her head, she decided to call one of her younger sisters.

"What's up Tania?" Tania was a sophomore in high school.

"Hey Teresa. Everything is okay, why didn't you call me back after I called two days ago?" Teresa had her moments when she would ignore her family to keep her sanity. They always had drama and always asked to borrow money that she really didn't have.

"Well, you know I be busy with school and work. Is everything good?" Teresa was hoping Tania didn't want anything.

"Honestly, everything isn't alright. Mama went missing for four days and when she finally returned, she was high off her ass. Teresa, she hasn't been doing too well. She's losing weight, won't eat much, walks around the house fussing and talking to herself, she's even started putting aluminum foil over the windows." Tania sounded concerned.

"Well, Ma has always fussed and did drugs, but it does sound like she's doing a little too much. Where is Dad? What does he have to say about all of this?" Their house was a mess growing up. Their dad was so nonchalant about everything and really let their mom control everything. It was ridiculous because she wasn't nurturing at all, she was actually hateful.

"Now you know Daddy hasn't said or done nothing. When she was missing, me and the boys kept asking about her and all he told us was she'll be back. That man didn't know where she was, and I don't even think he cared. Teresa, I had to cook, clean, and get the boys ready for school those days. No help from Daddy. The only thing he did was go to the store to pick up a few groceries. Then he's had his homeboys over here and one of them has been looking at me and winking at me." Tania knew her parents loved having company over but fucking with her siblings was off limits.

"What?! Is the dude over there now?" At that point, Teresa got hot again.

"Yes, he is, but they're all outside drinking beers." Tania responded.

"Bet, I'm on my way now!" Teresa didn't wait for a response, she hung up the phone and jumped in her car.

She arrived at her parents' house in ten minutes, ready to destroy everyone in sight. Before she confronted anyone, she went into the house to ask Tania which guy was violating her. Once Tania pointed him out, she grabbed a long, pointy kitchen knife. She stormed outside and grabbed the disgusting predator by his hair, held his head down, and placed the tip of the knife to his neck. "Listen to me, you piece of shit! If I ever hear anything else about you or any of these old motherfuckers out here looking at, talking to, or touching any of my siblings, I will end you!" She dug the knife into his neck with just enough pressure to draw blood. Teresa was past the stage of fearing for her own life. After enduring her childhood pain and trauma, nothing scared her. She looked around and dared anyone to say something. Even her dad was afraid to speak. He was a spineless man and didn't even have the guts to reiterate her threat to his so-called friends. She finally released the geezer and stormed back in the house to look for her useless mother.

"Tasha!!! Where you at Ma?" She went to her mother's bedroom to find her balled up on the floor. She smelled horrific. "Ma you need to get up! You smell and look terrible. You have three more kids in this house that you're supposed to be raising.

Get up!" She started shaking her mom and pulling on her arm to motivate her to move.

"Then Daddy's nasty ass friends out there looking at Tania like she's a piece of meat! Y'all need to get this together over here. I'm trying to work and put myself through school, I can't keep coming to YOUR kids rescue while you decide to do drugs!" Teresa stopped trying to budge her mom and dropped to the floor beside her. She started crying. How could her family be so fucked up? Her mom had been on drugs for years and even lost custody of children behind her drug addiction. Teresa had never seen her mom this bad.

As hateful as her mom had been towards her, it broke her heart to see her like this. She called Tania in the room and asked her to help walk their mom into the bathroom. It took a little work to get their mom up; it was really difficult lifting someone's entire weight. Once they were in the bathroom, Teresa ran some bath water and placed her mom in the tub. She let her sit there for close to ten minutes so she could soak. Her skin looked filthy, covered in dirt and blood.

"Ma, what happened to you while you were missing?" Teresa asked.

"Girl, please leave." Tasha managed to slur those words while keeping her eyes closed.

"No, I'm not leaving until I get you cleaned up. You look and smell disgusting." Teresa didn't mind talking to her mom in any kind of way now. She was no longer a prisoner of her mom's abuse. She lived away from their house, she paid all of her bills, and she knew her true strength now. She was fully aware that her mom's brokenness could no longer control her. She was no longer a feeble child but instead a fearless young lady. She grabbed a washcloth and the small bar of soap that was in the tub. She began to wash her mother and started to hum 'When Doves Cry' by Prince. She started to get emotional and began singing the lyrics.

"How could you just leave me standing, lonely, the world is so cold." Tears began to stream down her face. She related so much to the lyrics of this song since her parents were very abusive and toxic. Tasha started to sing with Teresa. "Maybe I'm just like my mother, she's never satisfied. Why do we scream at each other? This is what it sounds like when the doves cry." Tasha started to cry too. Teresa was shocked to see her mom cry. She's never seen a soft side of her mom. She knew that her mom loved Prince and his music but never imagined that she would get emotional.

"What's wrong Ma?" Teresa asked.

"I have failed all of you. I failed y'all." Tasha sobbed as she placed her face in her hands. Teresa stopped bathing her mom and wrapped her arms around her. She didn't care about getting the dirty water on her. At that point she just wanted to comfort her mom. Maybe this was a breakthrough for her. They sat in the bathroom and cried until Tania entered a few minutes later.

"What's going on?" Tania came in looking confused.

"I'm so sorry, Tania. I've been a terrible mom. I don't know what's wrong with me. I want to get clean, I really do. I don't want to be this demon to anyone. I don't want to be selfish. I really want to get my life together. I promise, I DO! GOD PLEASE HELP!" Tasha expressed herself. Her daughters just sat there and listened to their mom cry out for help.

Tasha explained how she was introduced to drugs at a young age by one of the neighborhood pimps growing up. She was outside one day when the ice cream truck came by. The pimp named Dale asked if she wanted anything from the truck and she told him she did but didn't have any money. Dale told her not to worry about anything, that he would pay for whatever she wanted. Like any vulnerable child, Tasha went along with him. That behavior continued for a few weeks, until the pimp invited her out for pizza. She looked up to Dale as a father figure. Tasha had lost her dad to heart disease when she was just eight years old. At the age of thirteen, she looked very mature, but mentally, she was innocent. The day she went out for pizza, Dale offered her a piece of candy that would make her happy. At first, she was hesitant, but she trusted Dale. He always looked out for her, so she knew he'd never do anything to hurt her. What Tasha didn't know was that Dale preyed on girls like her. She didn't have a father figure around and her mom worked long hours.

After that day, Dale had Tasha hooked on ecstasy. She would consistently ask him for the 'special candy'. Dale saw the effect the drugs had on Tasha and knew it was time for him to introduce her to a new lifestyle. One day after school, Dale rolled up on Tasha in his Oldsmobile as she was walking home. She was excited to see him since she knew she'd get some special candy. Dale told her to get in the car to ride with him. Tasha complied, and they rode a few blocks down to an apartment. Starting from that, Tasha sold her body in exchange for drugs. She started out on ecstasy and eventually went on to harder drugs, such as cocaine and heroin. By Tasha's fourteenth birthday, she was strung out. Her mom was distraught and didn't know what to do with her. She attempted to send Tasha to live with her paternal grandparents in San Diego, California, but Tasha started to run away. Her family couldn't help her. She only wanted to be around Dale and the drugs. Fast forward twenty-five years later, and Tasha was still hooked. She tried to shake the drugs several times but only managed to be clean during her pregnancies.

"Ma, I never knew all of this." Teresa was in shock and couldn't believe that her mom's drug addiction began at such an early age.

"It's ridiculous that Dale's grown ass took advantage of you like that." Tania was infuriated.

"It's okay. I'm going to get clean. I'm serious this time, and I'm ready. I have to get better for all eight of my kids. I know I don't show it, but I love all of y'all and I'm proud. Teresa, I'm really sorry for the way I've treated you. I'm sorry I was a shitty mom. I'm sorry I haven't been able to help you with school. I don't deserve such an intelligent, hardworking daughter. You've always cared for your siblings and done my job. This was my last time getting high." Tasha cried.

Once they got their mother out of the tub and dressed, they placed her in bed in front of a heater. Tasha complained about being cold. The girls left her alone to go research drug rehabilitation places nearby. They found a place called Good Landing Recovery which was located about an hour away from them. That was the perfect place for Teresa to take her mom. It was close enough for Teresa and her siblings to go visit, but far enough for her mom to not know anyone. Teresa went outside to talk to her dad to tell him what was going on.

"Pops, can you come here for a second?" Teresa yelled over the voices and music playing in the background.

"Shit, hold on y'all, let me go talk to my sweet daughter right quick." He walked over to Teresa and all of his friends were staring, all except the one she pulled the knife on. They looked timid and quickly turned their heads once she made eye contact.

"What's up baby girl?" Her dad asked.

"Tania and I got Mom cleaned up and in bed. We looked up a drug program for her and found a place out in the city of Dallas that's an hour away. I'm going to take her there tomorrow." Her dad cut her off by laughing.

"Teresa, your mom is a junkie, and she's been once since the day I met her. She'll never be anything other than that, so don't waste your time on that bitch." As soon as her dad uttered that curse word, Teresa slapped him clean across his face and spat at him.

"Nigga, you're one of the reasons she's stayed on the drugs! You supplied her for a long time and never ever tried to motivate her to get clean! Don't you ever talk down on her as if you're any better than she is, I'll fuck you up! Both of y'all have been jokes as parents, but for you to carry on like you're some kind of God or better than she is, is totally beyond me!" He held his face in disbelief that she had struck him and spoken to him in such a disrespectful way.

"Lil girl, you might be grown, but don't ever get shit twisted. I'll beat your ass like you stole something! You lucky all these people out here!" He snapped, looking around in anger and embarrassment.

"Nigga, I wish you would touch me. I'm not that little scared girl anymore. You don't run shit, and you're not tough. You think you're big and bad because you verbally and physically abuse women and kids. No sir, you're not. I've never seen you disrespect a man, even when they've disrespected you. You're pathetic, and I dare you to raise your hand to me. Your friends will have to call the DeKalb County Police Department to get me OFF YOU!" Teresa walked closer to him to show that she meant business. For the first time in her life, she stood up to her dad. They stared at each other until he walked away.

"Yeah, like I thought, pussy!" She grinned and it felt good. She knew he was a weak man who felt powerful by talking down to others. He walked back over to his friends, and they stood there quietly until Teresa left.

The next morning, Teresa pulled back up to her parents' house to get her mother. The door was unlocked as usual as she went inside to get her mom. She walked in the hallway to see her mom laying on the floor beaten and bruised. She instantly became furious and started looking around for her dad, but he was nowhere to be found, so she called his phone.

"Where the fuck are you?" she yelled.

"Little girl, don't call my phone with nonsense. What do you want?"

She replied, aggravated, "So you put your hands on my mom? I'm at your house looking for you so I can handle you." She spat at the phone in anger.

"Oh, you're back. Good, you don't have an audience today. I'll be there in two minutes." He hung up the phone. He pulled up a few minutes later, and Teresa was waiting for him outside. She was happy that her siblings were at school, she would hate for them to witness the ass whooping that she was about to hand to their dad.

"I see you're still here. I really don't want to hurt you, so you need to leave." Her dad chuckled as he tried to walk in the house. She didn't respond. Instead, she aggressively grabbed him by the arm to pull him back into the grass. Her dad stood 5 feet 6 inches to her 5 feet 4 inches. He was a lightweight, weighing no more than 160 pounds soaking wet. "Okay now, this is not what you want, Teresa. I'll have you looking like your mama." She landed a right jab in the middle of his face to connect with his nose. His groaned out in pain and attempted to grab her with both his arms, but she dodged him. She started hitting him with both her left and right fists until he lost his balance and fell on the ground. Once she saw him hit the ground, it was over. She began to kick him in his stomach and side. He balled up to cover his head, but that didn't stop her from stomping on top of his head. She was so angry, and all of her childhood memories popped up. She went to work on him for about two minutes until her mom came outside.

"Teresa, let it go. He's not worth it." She heard Tasha and stopped to turn around. Her mom was barely holding herself up as she leaned against the door frame.

"If I ever hear about your worthless ass laying a finger on my mom or ANY of my siblings again, I'll be back for some more!" She kicked him one last time before she helped her mom to the car. Once in the car, she looked at her dad who was still laying on the ground in pain. She felt relieved to have handled him, but she didn't think it would change his behavior.

An hour later, Teresa and Tasha arrived at the drug recovery center. They walked inside to a very tranquil environment. Teresa spoke with the inpatient doctor to get all of the paperwork filled out and to inform her of her mom's condition. Tasha sat in a chair looking frantic and terrible. Like many of the people who came there, she was in bad shape. The doctors and staff were accustomed to seeing that, and they assured Teresa that her mom would be in good hands. Shortly after finishing the paperwork, the ladies were given a tour and shown Tasha's living quarters. She was going to be in a room by herself due to

130

the severity of her addiction and her history of physical abuse.

"Hey Tasha, why don't you get settled in your room while I talk with your daughter for a second?" The nurse politely requested, and Tasha complied.

"Teresa, I want to thank you for having the courage to bring your mom to our facility. This is a big step, and she will one day appreciate you for this choice. Due to your mother's extensive drug history and her current condition, I want you to know that the minimum recommended time for her treatment is six months. We also recommend that she not have any visitors for her first month since her body will be going through a very heavy detox. Familiar people can trigger her desire to want to relapse. Since this is a voluntary admittance, your mom can leave at any time, unless there is some form of court documentation proving that she is a danger to herself or her kids. Do you have any other questions for me?" The nurse gave more pertinent details and had Teresa thinking. Teresa wanted to find a way to get a judge to require the treatment, but there was no way to get the courts involved without any police reports being filed. She just had to lean on faith and pray that her mom took her recovery seriously and would complete her treatment.

"No ma'am, you have done a great job explaining everything. I guess I'll go tell my mom before I leave." Teresa walked back into her mom's room to say her goodbyes.

"Well Ma, this looks like a really nice place. As you know, it is in your best interest to be here for six months. I really have faith that this is one of the best decisions you've ever made in your life. After your first month, I'm going to bring my siblings to see you, and we'll come every week after that. Despite everything that has gone on between us, I do truly love you and want the best for you. Please stay focused on your recovery and let these people help you. You deserve to be clean and healthy." Teresa stared at her mom with tears in her eyes. They embraced each other and hugged for close to a minute. They finally let go, and Teresa left her mother in her solitude. She was proud of her mom for taking this step. She had never seen her so vulnerable. When she got back to her car, she cried tears of joy. For once she felt like she actually bonded with her mom and that there was hope for a healthy relationship.

Eleven

Chapter 11

⚜

Jakeshia was wrapping up her fall semester finals when she got a call from Ms. Martha that Raoul was being released from the hospital. She wanted Jakeshia's help organizing Raoul's medication and medical supplies. At first, Jakeshia was hesitant because Ms. Martha's house always made Jakeshia feel at home, but she agreed. She had been very supportive of Raoul over the past few weeks and knew that her presence had been instrumental to his recovery. He was able to talk in full sentences without stuttering, he was walking slowly yet independent of all gait trainers, and a lot of his memory was returning. She was so proud of his progress. During her visits, Raoul kept things cordial and respected Jakeshia's boundaries. He stated how he understood that she had moved on and had a boyfriend. Occasionally, she would catch Ms. Martha grinning while she looked at them, but Ms. Martha kept her thoughts to herself. Jakeshia left school for her Christmas break and was confident that she had aced all of her finals. She knew the semester got her one step closer to becoming a nurse and was proud of her hard work despite all the obstacles.

She arrived at Ms. Martha's house with huge knots in her stomach. She hadn't spoken to Michael that day and was honestly afraid to tell him that she was going to help get Raoul situated. Her relationship was going great, but she could tell that Michael was getting annoyed with her assisting Raoul's recovery. Although Michael always said he understood, his body language said otherwise. "Hi Jakeshia! I'm so happy you could make it! Come on in." Jakeshia followed Ms. Martha into the guest room where Raoul was.

"Hey Keshia." Raoul looked excited to see her.

"Hey Raoul, so how does it feel to be back outside of the hospital?" she asked with a smile.

"It feels amazing. I am truly blessed and thankful for your and my mom's support. I feel really good right now considering the circumstances." They both smiled. Jakeshia followed behind Ms. Martha to help her unload various items out of boxes.

"Okay baby, so I'm not too handy. Do you think you can put this shelf together? The box says it's an easy build." Ms. Martha asked.

"I mean, I guess. It won't hurt to give it a try." Jakeshia went to work putting the shelf together, and it was an easy build. Once the shelf was put together, they began to place labels, medical supplies, and medication on the dividers.

"Ma, can you help me in the bathroom?" Raoul asked. Ms. Martha stopped working to help Raoul. Although he could walk independently, he still needed assistance with using the toilet and wiping himself. While they were in the bathroom, Jakeshia finished all the organizing. Once they returned, Jakeshia told them that she was heading out.

"Aw, so soon?" Raoul asked sadly.

"Yes. I have to get home and handle a few things." She was heading out the door when Raoul stood up and asked for a hug. She was hesitant at first but figured it wouldn't hurt anything. As she went for a hug, Raoul snuck a kiss on the lips. "Oh no, we can't do that." She stumbled backward and ran out of the house to her car.

She rode home in shame and disbelief. She was ashamed that she had allowed Raoul and Ms. Martha to guilt her into helping with his recovery. She was in disbelief that her feelings for him were resurfacing. While she drove home, Michael called, but she didn't have the courage to answer. She couldn't possibly tell him what just happened. Although it wasn't her fault, she was afraid that Michael would be upset with her and break things off. She was frustrated and decided to call her older sister Marissa. "Hey sis, what's up?" Marissa answered.

"Hey girl. I have a dilemma, and I need your advice." Jakeshia sighed. "I'm listening." Marissa replied.

"So, you know I've been going to the hospital these past few weeks to see Raoul. Today he got released and ended up going to Ms. Martha's. So she called me and wanted my help, so I agreed. This was a bad decision. When I got ready to leave, Raoul asked for a hug and stole a kiss." She told her story in a dramatic tone, to emphasize how serious the matter was.

"Giiirrrl, doesn't he know you have a man and don't want his dusty ass anymore? What the hell!" Her sister was irritated. She was not too fond of Raoul and liked Michael, even though she hadn't met him just yet.

"Exactly. I was being nice and trying to help him and Ms. Martha as he healed, but now I feel like a fool." She shook her head.

"Don't feel bad, sis. There's no way you would've known he would try that shit. I would just be done with him and keep it moving. I wouldn't even answer the phone for them anymore. You've wasted enough of your life on that jackass!" Marissa didn't care how ruthless she sounded.

"You're right. But now I'm wondering if I should tell Michael or not. I don't want him to get upset with me." Jakeshia was really scared of the possible outcome.

"Listen, you did nothing wrong. Tell him everything that happened and that you won't be involved in Raoul's life anymore. Based on everything you've told me about Michael, I feel like he will understand and really respect you for your honesty." They didn't always get along, but it was a good thing that Jakeshia could get some honest advice.

"Thank you, I'm going to give him a call and be honest." She felt a little relieved after having this conversation.

"Hey babe, I see you called." Jakeshia spoke in a sweet voice.

"Hey boo, how were your finals today?" Michael always called to check on her after school and work.

"You know I aced all of those. Soon you'll have to call me nurse Keshia." They both laughed. Before she spoke again, Jakeshia had to muster up the nerves to tell Michael about her day after school. She expressed to him that Ms. Martha called asking for her help with organizing.

"Okay, so are you headed over there now?" Michael asked.

"I'm on my way home. I just left. To be honest with you babe, I won't be involving myself with that dynamic anymore. When I was leaving, Raoul kissed me." She paused and waited for Michael's response. There was a short silence before Michael responded.

"So what did you do or say after he kissed you?" Michael asked.

"I immediately backed up and told him that we couldn't do any of that. I left immediately. I don't know what gave him the impression that he could try me like that. But again, I won't be helping out anymore or answering their calls." She was flustered as she expressed everything to Michael. She truly hoped that he wouldn't hold anything against her.

"Well Jakeshia, it's totally up to you whether or not you feel comfortable going over there or speaking to them. I know and trust that you haven't been leading him on. I appreciate you being honest with me about everything. Like I said from day one, I'm here to support you. I do feel as though you should at least answer the phone for them. Raoul hasn't been good to you all these years, but he did put himself in a situation where he is very vulnerable. If you completely ignore them, who knows what he is capable of doing. I just wouldn't want him to feel alone at this time." Damn! Michael was such a secure and thoughtful man. He knew he had his relationship on lock and that Jakeshia wasn't going anywhere. He didn't sound the slightest bit of upset.

"I understand where you're coming from. I guess I won't ignore them, but I will recommend that he start talking to a counselor. My friend Jamaal has been going to a male counselor who is based in Lithonia. He said he looks forward to every session." Jakeshia smiled and she thought about Jamaal and how proud she was of him for working on himself.

"Yeah, I think that will be a great idea. It's easy for us to cut people off but difficult to actually put effort into helping them grow. I'm not saying hold Raoul's hand through the process. It's just obvious to me that you have mad love for him, and I respect that, so there's nothing wrong with you helping him find other resources." They talked a little longer about different ways for Jakeshia to approach Ms. Martha and Raoul. They agreed that it would be best for her to no longer visit him, however she would answer their calls but limit her availability. Her time in his life was slowly but surely coming to an end. He would have to find a healthy way to accept that. To end their call, Michael reassured her that she was not at fault for anything that Raoul was going through.

The next day, Jakeshia called Michael to meet her for breakfast. Michael politely declined and instead sent her an address to meet him at. She was confused because he didn't give many details, but she got dressed and drove to the residence. She sat outside a beautiful colonial home. The yard was landscaped to perfection with azalea shrubs, colorful hydrangeas, and pink knot roses. There was the white picket fence and granite walkway. Jakeshia was in love with this house at first sight. Michael pulled up shortly after she did and walked up to open her car door to open it. They embraced each other in a long, warm hug. He smelled so good with his cologne, she wanted to eat him up.

"Hey boo, so where are we?" Jakeshia asked.

"You'll see in a second." Michael led her to the front door and rang the doorbell. They heard a voice on the other end sarcastically asking who was at the door. "It's me." Michael responded. They heard the door unlock before a beautiful young lady opened the door, cheesing extra hard. Michael introduced the girl as Grace.

"Hi Grace, it is so wonderful to finally meet you. Michael has told me so much about you." Jakeshia reached for a handshake, but Grace moved in for a hug.

"Girl, I have heard lots about you too. I feel like I already know you. You have my big brother smitten." Grace smiled as she looked over to Michael, who was blushing at the moment. "Come on, we're all in the den ready to eat!" Grace walked to the kitchen which was right next to the den. Their home had an open concept connecting the den, dining room, and kitchen. The kitchen was huge with plenty of counter space and stainless-steel appliances. After Jakeshia's quick glance of the kitchen, she looked over to the den to see the rest of Michael's family.

"Good morning fam. This is my girlfriend, Jakeshia." Michael grabbed her hand to acknowledge their unity. She felt so secure at this moment.

"Hi Jakeshia, I'm Olivia, Michael's mom. It is our pleasure to finally meet you. You're even more beautiful than he described." Mrs. Olivia came over to give her a welcoming hug. Immediately after, Miles and Liam introduced themselves. This family was full of hugs.

"Here, why don't you have a seat here while we go grab breakfast." Miles pulled out a chair for her while everyone else went to grab the eggs, sausage, grits, pancakes, toast, orange juice, and hash browns.

"This is a wonderful spread of food, and everything looks delicious. Thank you for having me in your home today." Although she was surprised at the visit, she was excited to finally meet Michael's family. This was a huge step. This truly showed her that Michael was serious and did not care about the drama she previously had with Raoul.

"Aww, you're welcome, sweetie. We have been hounding

Michael about bringing you by, but he insisted that you were busy working, going to school, and helping a friend. How is that friend of yours doing, by the way?" Mrs. Olivia asked with concern.

"He is doing much better. His condition has improved, and he's been released from the hospital." Jakeshia wanted to feel embarrassed, but it didn't appear that anyone knew the type of friend that Raoul was to her.

"That's great to hear. Everyone needs a friend like you. One who sticks around when times are good or bad. People like you are hard to come by. Michael, you better keep this one." Miles stated before asking everyone to join hands so he could bless the food.

They finished eating the delicious breakfast and went outside to their patio. The weather was a little chilly, but there was a heating lamp on the porch. Everyone sat at a table and agreed to play a few games. The first game they played was called Sequence. Miles and Olivia paired up, Liam and Grace paired up, and Jakeshia and Michael were in a team. "Jakeshia, have you played Sequence before?" Liam asked. This was apparently one of his favorite games.

"No, I've never even heard of this game before. How do I play?" Jakeshia asked inquisitively.

"So each of our teams will get a set of colored chips you place on the board and five cards to start out with. Each card in your hand will have a number and a symbol. You will simply play the card you want and place your chip on the replica that's on the board. Before your turn is over, you must pick up another card to replace the one you used. The team that gets two lines of five consecutive chips will win the round." Liam went on to tell her how she could remove someone else's chip and use the wild card.

"Oh yeah Michael, we definitely have this game in the bag. I used to kill it on Connect 4!" Everybody laughed at Jakeshia's confidence.

"Yeah babe, they just don't know that I have a mathematical genius in my hands." Michael emphasized Jakeshia's competitive spirit as he dealt everyone their cards. As the group played, Liam and Grace were the first team to get five cards in a row. Next Jakeshia and Michael were able to get their two lines off of one final play to win the first round.

"Now that's what I like to call beginner's luck!" Miles said while side-eyeing Jakeshia.

"I'm sorry Mr. Miles, but I already warned you all that your girl has skills!" Jakeshia said with a smirk. The group played Sequence, Phase 10, and Uno for the next three hours. There was an abundance of laughter, jokes, clean name calling, and plenty of card slapping on the table. "This has been a really fun morning and afternoon. I thank you all for being so hospitable and being good sports as I whooped butt." Jakeshia laughed as everyone walked back into the house.

"Oh darling, it was surely our pleasure to have you. You are welcomed here anytime, even without Michael." Olivia smiled as she hugged Jakeshia's shoulder.

"Thank you, I will definitely be back soon." Michael grabbed their coats and headed towards the door. Everyone hugged Michael and Jakeshia before they exited through the front door. "Your family is amazing. Is everyone always this nice and energetic?" Jakeshia asked as they stood by her car door.

"Yes, they are. To be honest, they can be more rowdy than that." They both laughed.

"That's what's up. This really does explain why you are the man you are. Always calm, caring, outgoing, intelligent, thoughtful, and your physical appearance is just the icing on the cake. I'm going to take your mom up on her offer soon. I love it here." Jakeshia smiled as she looked back to the beautiful house.

"You are truly welcomed to come with me every time. And I'm looking forward to meeting your family one day when you're ready." Michael grabbed her hands as he admired her beauty.

"Well, I may be able to make that happen. My mom works a lot, but she'll definitely be off for Christmas. We'll see." She winked at Michael. They talked a little longer before they jumped in their cars to go their separate ways. As Jakeshia drove off, she was genuinely happy thinking about how life could be having Michael's family as her in-laws.

Twelve

Jamaal's Story

~~~~~~~~~

"Hey, what's crackin' Keshia?" Jamaal was on his way to see Dr. G when he got a call from Jakeshia.

"Heeyyy Jamaal. Long time, no hear, my friend. How are you doing?" Jamaal hadn't really spoken to Jakeshia since he disclosed that he had feelings for her. They had made small talk here and there, but he was too embarrassed to face her after that day. "I'm honestly doing so much better since the last time you saw me. I have been really consistent with seeing Dr. Vaughn Gay. I almost feel like a new person. This brother really gets me. He's never experienced my struggle with the war, but he has tapped into my brain and helped me understand how to deal with my trauma in ways that are emotionally healthy for me. Enough about me though, how are you?" Jamaal could talk about Dr. G all day if she let him.

"I'm super glad to hear that. I was honestly calling you to ask about your counselor. As you know, Raoul shot himself in the head a few months ago, and I wanted to get him in contact with a good counselor." Jakeshia explained.

"Oh yeah, I'll give you his information and tell him to be on the lookout. So, are you and Raoul back on good terms?" Jamaal sounded a little jealous.

"No. I am happy with Michael. I do still have much love for Raoul and want to see him be his best self. I gave support to him through his hospital journey, but I think this will be my last gesture. I don't want him to get the wrong idea, and I'm not trying to mess up what I'm building with Michael." Jakeshia explained.

"I understand that. Well, I'm happy to hear that. I just pulled up to Dr. G's office, so I'll text you his info and talk to you later. Enjoy the rest of your day, it was good hearing from you." They said their goodbyes and hung up the phone.

Jamaal walked into Dr. G's office and felt like the man. Dr. G made him feel empowered, knowledgeable, strong, and almost fearless. He spoke life into him as a big brother would and reinforced the reality that men hurt and cried. Dr. G was not only an agent of change but a teacher throughout their sessions. He taught Jamaal how to experience his emotions while still conquering his everyday tasks. "What's up Doc?!" They both smiled as they engaged in a handshake.

"Aww, nothing much, man. Just handling a few invoices in between clients. Let's head on back. How's your day going so far?" Dr. G was always cool and swagged out. He had a slender frame and stood over six feet tall. He always wore nice slacks with the cleanest dress shoes. Jamaal peeped his style every time and knew he had to up his wardrobe game.

"I'm doing good. My homegirl just gave me a call and asked about you. One of her ex-boyfriends who is going through some things should be reaching out to you soon." Jamaal took a seat in the chaise. He loved how he could relax at an incline while looking up to the ceiling to express his thoughts.

"Thank you for the referral. I'm always accepting new clients, especially young brothers. You know where I'm from, black men are taught to not express their emotions. I'm on a mission to change that. As a matter of fact, I've been thinking about doing this free 12-week program for ten men. In this program, we will come together to talk about our mental health, work on building different communication skills, and do some community service." Dr. G passed Jamaal a flyer that he'd been working on.

"Oh, this is dope Doc. I'd be down to join. We need more opportunities like this. As you said, we weren't taught to express ourselves let alone how to feel emotions. Many of us definitely weren't taught how to effectively communicate." Jamaal looked over the flyer with a smile. He admired the fact that Dr. G was always engaged in doing work in the community. Although time was money, Dr. G made sure he invested time to give back to men and women who could benefit from his expertise.

"So tell me, what's new since the last time we met." Dr. G put on his glasses and pulled out his notepad to begin taking notes.

"Where do I start?" Jamaal chuckled and went on to tell Dr. G about how he had gone out with a few friends the other day. They were at a bar, and he approached a female that he found attractive. "This Jawn was a solid ten, Doc. She was curvy, hair laid, natural beauty with no makeup, very poised and classy, and she was dressed real nice. From her appearance, she had it all. I spoke with her for a few minutes and got her number. I hit her up the following day and asked to take her to lunch at Morton's Steakhouse, you know, nothing too fancy." Jamaal paused and laughed along with Dr. G.

"Hold on man, nothing too fancy? Boy, Morton's is definitely upscale and not cheap. I see you pulled out all the stops for this young lady. She sounds like a beauty." Dr. G smiled and nodded his head.

"My words can't even express how strikingly gorgeous this lady is. We went for lunch and her conversation was amazing. I honestly don't think I would've been prepared to start dating again if it wasn't for these sessions." Jamaal expressed himself with a genuine smile on his face.

"Well, I'm very proud of you. I'm just assisting in your journey brother, you already possess the necessary skills to be a great suitor." The two continued to talk about Jamaal's lunch date and how he has continued to develop his friendship with his new lady friend. "Sounds like good stuff, man. Just take things slow and never be afraid to communicate your thoughts or feelings. I've found that women want to be heard and they want to engage in productive dialogue. You can't win in any relationship when you're hiding your true thoughts. If she's doing things that make you happy, express it and give her compliments. Whenever her actions aren't favorable, respectfully express those feelings as well. You never want to hold things in, that can build up disdain or anger within you. You may be afraid of how she will react, but a partner worth building with will always take heed and consider your valid feelings."

Jamaal was amazed at the wisdom he was receiving. Dr. G named his practice 'Holistic Atlanta' for a reason. You really received the treatment for your whole mind. Jamaal came to counseling to deal with his post-traumatic stress disorder, but he was also being coached to become a better man all around. This was one of the best investments he's made into his life.

"Thanks G, I really needed that. Growing up with just my mom, I wasn't taught how to be a man, let alone someone's potential husband." They got into the topic of Jamaal's overall mental state and coping with his PTSD. Over the past few months, he has gone from being frightened by loud noises and lights, to sleeping peacefully at night. He hadn't broken down and cried in a few weeks, and that was really major. Seeing children, men, and women die in front of him had him so heartbroken.

Thanks to counseling, he wasn't numb to the pain but understood that the previous events were completely out of his control. Counseling had conditioned his mind and heart to feel emotions, cry, and move forward with life. He understood that crying was not a weak emotion, but it actually showed strength to have empathy for others.

"Jamaal, I'm proud of all of your work and improvement. I think you have elevated to a point where we can decrease the number of sessions you have each month." Jamaal had been seeing Dr. G once a week. "What do you think about coming every other week?" Dr. G posed their new schedule.

"I think that will be cool. You're the specialist, and I trust your judgement." Jamaal respected Dr. G and knew he had his best interest at hand.

"Sounds like a plan, my man. My goal is to heal you and water your growth. I don't ever want my clients to need me or become dependent on my services." The two got up and walked to the front lobby making small talk.

"Alright G. So, I guess I'll be seeing you in two weeks?" Jamaal edged into his question about their new meeting schedule.

"Yes sir, I will see you in two weeks. You take care brother." They gave each other a handshake with a brotherly hug.

"Good afternoon, gorgeous. How is your day going?" Jamaal called Denise, his female friend he had met at the bar.

"Hi handsome! My day is going well. I'm so happy you called me. I have to tell someone about this amazing client I had this morning." Denise was a hairdresser who was a co-owner of a salon in downtown Atlanta.

"What happened?" Jamaal loved that they could talk like good friends as if they knew each other for years.

"So this lady who found my information online walked in today, and she wanted a simple wash and style. As I was doing her hair, we were talking, and she began to tell me about her husband who is an executive director for the operations of the Phillips Arena. With his position, he is over all the managers for literally every single department there. She loved her hair so much that she wanted to refer him to me so that I may be a contractor when they need an in-house stylist for certain events!!!" Denise sounded so excited about this potential opportunity. She was twenty-two, so a few years older than Jamaal, but she was definitely on her grind. At times, Jamaal felt like she was out of his league with her owning a business and her own home. But Denise always assured him that she really admired his character and personality.

"Wow! That is phenomenal! This could really open up doors for you. I'm proud of you D. It's crazy that we haven't known each other that long, but in this small amount of time I can truly say that I see your ambition and hunger to be better. You motivate me when you don't even try to."

Denise had a rough childhood growing up. She was moved from foster home to foster home. She didn't know either of her biological parents, nor did she have any information about them. She grew up in Cameron, South Carolina and decided to move to Atlanta after her eighteenth birthday. Since she was an orphan, she was able to get a scholarship for cosmetology schools. She only had to worry about finding a place to stay and securing a part time job. While she was in school the government also gave her a monthly allowance to go towards her housing. After a year and a half in Georgia, she finished school and was able to find a job in a salon. Once she built up her clientele and reputation, she had enough money to go off with another stylist to open up their salon. Denise was living proof of a person who went from rags to riches.

She was determined to never allow her broken childhood to keep her from excelling as an adult. Denise was always mistreated by people, even in her 20s. The men who approached her seemed to only want her for her physical beauty, that was until Jamaal walked into her life. Jamaal was different. He showed interest in Denise's career, hobbies, past, and her desires. Jamaal gave her hope that good men did exist and that she may actually get married one day. Growing up in the foster care system, she never knew love nor tender care from anyone, so all of this good attention was new to her, but she loved it.

Jamaal set up another date with Denise. For the first time, he was going to be picking her up from her house. He arrived at her place around 6:30 p.m., since he had made a reservation for 7:00 p.m. He parked the car, walked to her door, and rang the doorbell. He had been talking to Dr. G and receiving pointers about how to be chivalrous. Denise came to the door wearing a pair of skintight burgundy leather pants, a black blouse, with a black fedora, and a pair of black heels. Jamaal's mouth immediately dropped. This woman was the shit! "Good evening, beautiful. I feel underdressed; you look like you're ready to go hit the runway." Jamaal handed her the bouquet of roses.

"Aww, these are for me? Thank you, they are stunning! And thanks for the compliment, you know I try to throw a little somethin' somethin' on every now and then." Denise took the flowers and sat them on a coffee table in her living room before she exited the house.

"The exterior of your home is nice by the way." He put his hand out to help her down the steps as he led her to his car.

"Thank you. This will be one of my first investments. I'll rent it out or sell it once I can afford my dream home." Denise may have grown up in the foster system, but she was a straight A student. She did all of her schoolwork, plus read additional books from the school library. One book she read was about financial literacy and becoming your own boss.

"I see I have a lot to learn from you." Jamaal chuckled as he opened the car door for Denise.

"We have a lot to learn about and from each other. Everyone in your life, whether young or old, has something to teach you. I can't remember where I read that, but that saying has stuck with me for years." Denise fastened her seat belt as she got ready for the ride. "So where are you taking me?" she asked.

"We actually have two destinations. We'll be going to eat, then I have an activity for you. I hope you can move like Jagger in those heels!" They both bust out laughing.

"I don't know about all of that, but I'll try." Denise started to do the Bankhead bounce to the beat of the music on the radio.

"Oh snap. What you know about the Bankhead bounce? You an Atlanta vet now! It's stamped!" Jamaal exclaimed as he was impressed with her moves.

Denise and Jamaal pulled into the parking lot of Fogo De Chao near Perimeter mall and stopped at the valet. "Okay, so you're trying to get me fat? I see what we're doing here." Denise joked. The two went inside and were sat by the hostess immediately upon entering. They both ordered water with lemon and placed their cards on green to receive meat. Fogo De Chao was not your typical restaurant. It was a Brazilian steakhouse where different servers came around with types of meat. The servers shaved meat on your plate if it was the type of meat that you desired. They served all you could eat pork, beef, chicken, and lamb. They also had a market table with vegetables, bread, cheese, fruit, and soup. The two enjoyed multiple pieces of all the meats that were served, salad, bread, and asparagus. After eating for an hour, Jamaal was stuffed.

"Hold on now, save your appetite for dessert." Jamaal rubbed his belly as he looked across the table at Denise, who was buttering a roll.

"Listen sir, a girl can eat. You know I expend so many calories from standing at work and going to the gym. Don't worry, this body will still be right and tight." Denise laughed as she took a bite from her buttered roll.

"Yeah, you definitely look perfect just the way you are." Jamaal leaned to the side of the table to get a view of her body.

"Stooopp, don't make me blush up in here." Denise smiled. The two declined dessert, Jamaal paid for their food, and they headed out to the valet area. "So where to next?" Denise asked.

"Be patient, love. You'll see very soon." Jamaal put the car in drive then pulled off.

About ten minutes later, they arrived at Atlanta 360, which was a bowling alley nearby. "Oh, so you had plans to get your ass kicked at bowling today?!" Denise stated while nodding her head.

"I was always taught to let a lady win, but the way you talking... I don't know about taking it easy." Jamaal got out of the car to go open the door for Denise.

"Man, I will beat you with my heels on! Just watch me work!" Denise stepped out of the car and did a quick two step to show Jamaal that she could move in her heels.

"I hear you, miss lady. I don't want you to hurt nothing though, so you may want to trade those heels in for some bowling shoes. You know the floor is slippery." The two walked into the building, and Jamaal gave the associate his name. He had already reserved a lane for them.

"Okay then, I see you already had this thing planned out. I like!" Denise was impressed.

"Well, you know, I did have it planned to bowl and have a good time with you. Now I did not plan the hurtin' I'm bout to put on you." Jamaal smiled as he grabbed Denise's hand to lead her to their lane. "Ladies first, my dear." Jamaal entered both their names and assigned Denise to be the first player.

"That's not a problem at all. Let me show you how it's supposed to be done." Denise winked at Jamaal as she walked up to the line to bowl. She stepped with her opposite foot, swung her right arm back and forth three times, then released the ball forward. She knocked down eight pins on her first roll. "One more roll to go." She waited for her ball to be returned before she walked back to the line. Seconds later, she rolled a spare.

"Uh oh, looks like I'm in trouble." Jamaal said as he got up to give Denise a high five.

"You definitely are in trouble. I guess you can say I'm the one taking it easy on you. Just imagine how I'd bowl without the heels." Denise sashayed over to the chairs to take a seat. Jamaal hit three pins on his first roll and two on his second. Denise just looked at him and tried to hold in her laughter, but once he turned around, she couldn't help herself. "Jamaaaal you do not have to play like an amateur. I want to beat you fair and square." She got up and gently massaged his shoulders.

"Trust me, I'm being serious. I just need to warm up a little bit. Don't worry." Jamaal stated as he gazed into Denise's eyes. The two bowled for about an hour with the lead changing three times throughout the ten frames. By the end of the game, Denise clutched the win by hitting three strikes in the tenth frame.

"Damn D! You really know how to bowl! And you beat me while wearing heels. I can't tell the guys about this one." Jamaal laughed as they walked out of the bowling alley.

"I told you I would whoop your tail! I don't play any games boo. I'll give you a run for your money at anything competitive." The two laughed as they got into the car. This night made Jamaal like Denise even more.

Jamaal was determined to get his life back on track. He was coping with his post war trauma, getting out of the house more, and even exploring his admiration for Denise. The only thing that Jamaal needed to work on was getting back into the workforce. He was confused about what he wanted to do, but he knew he was not going back into the service or reserves. Since he was discharged due to an injury, he was still receiving a partial pay of eighty percent of his salary, and if he decided to go to school, the G.I. bill would pay for school. After talking to Denise and Jakeshia he decided to make an appointment with an educational advisor at Georgia State University. All of this was new to him, so he again found himself nervous. College was a totally different ball game from grade school. Before he headed out of the door, he grabbed a notebook and a pencil. He wanted to be sure that he took notes as he spoke with the advisor.

After driving for twenty-five minutes, Jamaal arrived at his appointment on time. He sat in the waiting room patiently until his name was called. About five minutes later, he was met by a beautiful advisor who introduced herself as Tameka. Tameka stood about 5'3 with a very curvaceous body. She directed him to follow her into her office, where he sat in front of a computer. "Okay Jamaal, on the screen there will be a few questions for you to answer. Once you have completed the questionnaire, there will be some careers generated based on your answers. We will discuss those careers and go from there." She has the prettiest voice, but Jamaal told himself that he was only there for business purposes. He proceeded to answer the questions, which took about fifteen minutes. Once he was done, he informed Tameka.

"Okay, so let me see what careers are compatible with your personality and interest. So, you have five very strong matches. Computer engineering, plumbing, HVAC, marketing, and business management. Based on these five things, can you pinpoint which one you may have a passion for?" Tameka read over his results and inquired about his preference.

"Can you explain HVAC to me?" Jamaal did not have a clue what HVAC stood for.

"Sure. HVAC is short for heating, ventilation, and air conditioning. People who work in this field visit different homes and businesses to fix or install the heating or air conditioning systems that move the air between indoors and outdoors." Tameka was very knowledgeable about the different career paths that the test generated. She told Jamaal that she had been working for Georgia State for seven years.

"Okay. Out of those five, I could see myself doing plumbing or HVAC. Which one gets paid the most?" Jamaal chuckled but he was serious about his question. "A person working in HVAC is estimated to make $28,000-$52,000 a year, while a person working as a plumber has an estimated income of $30,000-$60,000 a year." Tameka printed out the fact sheets for both careers and handed the sheet to Jamaal. The fact sheet included the amount of time it would take to get licensed in those fields, the estimated pay rate, as well as the subprograms that Georgia State provided. Jamaal looked them over and decided that he would do some more research while at home. He thanked Tameka for her time and got ready to leave her office.

"Jamaal before you leave, here's my card. You can call me anytime if you want more information or if you just want to talk." She winked and smiled seductively as he exited her office. Jamaal was flattered by her advance, but he was too smitten by Denise to ever take Tameka up on her offer.

Thirteen

Chapter 13

Jakeshia was finishing her senior year in nursing while attending Emory University. She had transferred to Emory University during her junior year and loved her transition. Emory had the best clinical experiences, was well known, and provided her with financial aid to complete her bachelor's in nursing. Their program was rigorous, but she was able to train with some of the top doctors in the United States. "Jakeshia, can you hand me a bag of IV fluid?" Jakeshia was training in the emergency room at Emory hospital for the next few weeks. She loved medicine, but the worst part of being in the ER was when people came in with detached or missing body parts. The patient they were currently treating had been admitted after fainting. Jakeshia checked the patient and determined that the lady was dehydrated and was in need of further tests to see what may have caused the dehydration and fainting. The nurse that she was shadowing put in an order for blood work to be taken, and that was the first step to determining the lady's underlying issues. After Jakeshia passed the IV fluid over to the nurse, she looked at her watch to see that her shift was over. Although some nurses and doctors worked overtime, during her clinical hours she only worked 4-6 hours a day. She still had to do schoolwork and study. Once she left the hospital, she had a dinner date with Michael, but he hadn't expressed where they were headed.

Jakeshia arrived at her house around 6 p.m. She was exhausted from her school/work week but was excited to meet with Michael. She ran a bubble bath to relax her body. Michael was coming to pick her up at 7 p.m., so she figured she had enough time to meditate and listen to a little old school R&B. As she ran her bath water, 'Sweet Love' by Anita Baker began to play on the V103 radio station. She dropped her clothes on the bed and started to dance to the sultry song. "Never leave, cause baby I believe in this love!" She sang her heart out as if Michael was in the room. She swayed her hips and she sashayed to the tub.

While she was in the tub, she reminisced on how much her and Michael's relationship had blossomed in the two years they had been dating. Shortly after she met Michael's family, she invited him over for Christmas at her mom's. He was able to meet both of her sisters and two of her brothers. He really hit it off with her siblings, who were all welcoming. Michael even made her mom laugh, which was a plus since her mom rarely interacted with Jakeshia's friends or boyfriends. Her family absolutely hated Raoul, so they were rooting for her relationship with Michael. She was definitely sweet on Michael and decided to cut all ties with Raoul after she referred him to Dr. G. She always repeated the saying, "If nothing changes, nothing changes." She knew that Raoul would never change as long as she was a crutch for him. She also realized that it was not her job to save anyone, except the patients she cared for at the hospital.

BUUZZZZ!!! Jakeshia's phone woke her up from her bathtub daze. She grabbed the phone to see it was Michael calling. "Hey babe, what are you doing?" Michael asked.

"Hey boo! I'm just in the tub getting ready for tonight." She looked at her phone to see the time, and 45 minutes had passed while she was daydreaming.

"Great. I'll be there at 7:30 sharp! I want you to wear that purple dress that I bought you two weeks ago." Michael was making a special request. She wondered if he wanted her to match his fly that day.

"Okay babe, I'll wear whatever you want me to, included." They both laughed and made small talk the next few minutes until Jakeshia exited the tub. She went to her closet and grabbed the purple dress, a pair of black heels to match, and silver accessories. She placed the item on her bed and moisturized with some Olay body lotion. Once she got dressed, she finalized her look with a spray of Bath and Body Works sweet pea body spray. She looked over at the clock on her night stand, and it read 7:28 p.m. She went ahead and walked downstairs to the front door and peeked outside to see Michael's car. She loved that he was a man of his word, he said 7:30 p.m. and he meant it! Jakeshia walked outside and Michael immediately hopped out of his car to go give her the biggest hug and a juicy kiss.

"Damn you look beautiful!" Michael grabbed her hand and twirled her around to get a complete view of her body.

"Aww, thank you my love." Jakeshia smiled from ear to ear. The dress fit her body like a glove. Michael opened the car door for her and stared at her one last time before he closed the door. At that moment, he knew he would be the luckiest man on Earth by the end of the night.

They arrived at Two Urban Licks close to 8:00 p.m. and were greeted by the valet. Michael escorted her inside where she saw many familiar faces. She was growing suspicious about her family and Michael's family being present. It wasn't anyone's birthday, Valentine's Day had passed already, and graduation was a month or so away. She waved and hugged their loved ones as she made her way to the two empty chairs. "Michael, what is all this about?" Before Michael could respond, the singer Lloyd walked around the corner singing Musiq Soulchild's 'Love'.

"Loooove, there's so many things I've got to tell you, but I'm afraid I don't know how…" She was star struck at the moment. Jakeshia placed her hand over her mouth and tried to contain her excitement. Michael knew she loved Lloyd. She even ran into him at Stonecrest mall years ago and took a picture with him. She was so into Lloyd and his singing that she totally overlooked Michael, who was on the other side of her on one knee. Her mom grabbed her attention and told her to look the other way. When Jakeshia turned her head, she squealed out loud, so loud that everyone in the restaurant could probably hear her. She got up out of her chair and stood directly in front of Michael, who had shed a tear. Seeing him so emotional instantly brought tears to her eyes. She really loved Michael and was in total awe at this proposal. Lloyd stopped singing, and Michael began a speech.

"Jakeshia, from the moment I laid eyes on you at Spelman, I

159

knew you were the one. Just looking at you, I knew you were not only beautiful, but you also carried grace. You are a lover of all, you're outgoing, your ambition is something I've never seen from anyone else, you're firm and don't take anyone's shit. Everyone literally tells me how lucky I am to have you, and I agree one thousand percent. You make loving you so easy, and I couldn't wait another day without coming to you and asking you to be my wife. So, Jakeshia, will you marry me?" Michael had shed even more tears during his speech, and almost everyone at the table was crying.

"Yes, yes I will marry you!!! Oh my god, I can't believe this is happening to me!" Jakeshia wiped her face and embraced Michael as he got up from kneeling on one knee. As the two hugged and kissed, everyone in the restaurant was clapping and cheering them on. Michael was surely the luckiest man on Earth once Jakeshia agreed to marry him.

The next few days, Jakeshia was on cloud nine. Her 10-karat ring was so huge. Michael had gotten his degree in engineering the previous summer and was offered a job right before he graduated. He was working 40 hours a week and making $75,000 with full benefits. With his company, he was eligible for raises at random times throughout the year. He had received his first raise around Valentine's Day and knew then that he was going to buy Jakeshia the biggest diamond ring he could afford.

After the proposal dinner, Michael had whisked her away for a weekend in Blue Ridge at a mountain cabin. They were in a 2-bedroom, 2-bathroom cabin that had a Jacuzzi, pool table, and sat in front of a lake. They enjoyed watching the sun rise and set from the balcony of their bedroom. They even made love on the balcony their first night there. She was not ready to leave and go back to school, but she was so close to becoming a nurse and would finish strong. She had a 4.0 GPA and was top of her class. Many of her fellow classmates came to her for help on assignments, and she always made herself available to help. Once she started her clinical experience, she quit her job at Arizona's to focus solely on school. She had saved up a lot of money and planned on paying her bills with her savings, but Michael stepped in and took full responsibility for her bills. She was so blessed and grateful for the role that Michael played in her life. He added value to the woman she was and also provoked her to grow into a better woman. She was ready to see what life would be like after her proposal weekend.

"Okay class, so if you see someone laying on the ground and they seem to be unconscious, what is the first thing you should do?" Jakeshia's professor was going over the proper first aid and CPR protocol. Jakeshia raised her hand to answer. "I should first check the scene to make sure it is safe, then if it's safe I will approach the individual and ask if they are okay while tapping them on the shoulder." Jakeshia knew the steps like the back of her hand. This was her last day of class before they took their live finals. For the live finals, she had to present a project outlining the medical supplies needed to check vital signs and administer medicine to a patient with hypoglycemia. There was also a written test that she would have three hours to complete. She was nervous and excited at the same time. Once they finished the review, her professor called her over to his desk.

"Hey Jakeshia, I just want to congratulate you on maintaining your 4.0 GPA throughout your four years on the nursing path.

I received an email yesterday from Dr. Jones which expressed that Emory Hospital is interested in hiring you immediately after you walk across the stage next week." He proceeded to hand a printed copy of the job offer over to Jakeshia, who was gleaming in gratitude.

"Oh wow, this is a dream come true! Thank you so much for your mentorship, I couldn't have been this knowledgeable without you. I will look this over once I get home." Jakeshia left the classroom cheerfully yet humble.

As she walked towards her car, her phone rang. It was Raoul. What could he possibly have wanted? She hadn't spoken to him in damn near a year. He had fully recovered from the injuries he sustained in his suicide attempt. "Hello." Jakeshia answered the phone with a perplexed tone.

"Hey Keshia, how are you?" Raoul asked.

"I'm well, just heading home to go study for my finals tomorrow." She wanted to end the call as quickly as possible. She didn't wish to be rude, but Raoul was a thing of the past.

"That's what's up. I just wanted to call and congratulate you on your recent engagement. Bear told me his wife ran into you at the store the other day. I hear your ring is massive." Raoul actually sounded happy for her.

"Well, thank you. Yes, I got engaged to Michael about a month ago." Jakeshia smiled all over again thinking about her engagement.

"That's what's up. I'm happy for you." This was surprising coming from him.

"Thank you. How has everything been going for you?" Jakeshia asked.

"You know, everything is finally falling into place. I have been meeting with Dr. G consistently and battling my depression. He got me to open up about…" Raoul paused as he gathered his thoughts. "He finally got me to open up about being molested and raped when I was younger." Jakeshia gasped in sympathy.

"Raoul, I never knew that. I'm so sorry to hear that. I'm happy that you are able to unpack that trauma." Jakeshia felt bad that he carried this burden for such a long time.

"It's okay. I want to genuinely apologize for the way I treated you back then. I didn't know how to deal with women. I expressed my pain through being a womanizer, and Dr. G is really helping me become a better man for my future. I do thank you for connecting me to him. And thank you for always showing me real love. Your fiancé is a lucky guy. I just wish I was able to be the man you needed when I had the opportunity." Raoul was very expressive all of a sudden. Receiving counseling allowed him to see where he went wrong in his life. He was able to appreciate everyone who loved him and tried to help him. He still had demons to fight, but he was headed in the right direction.

"Well, I appreciate the compliment and wish you the best with everything in life. I believe you will one day meet another woman who is good to you, I just hope that you are ready to receive and value her when you do meet her. Have a great day, I'm getting in my car and heading home now." Jakeshia didn't want to be rude, but the conversation was over at that point.

"Thank you for taking the time out to talk to me. I wish you well, Jakeshia." Raoul sounded sad as they hung up the phone. She didn't want to delve too much into the past. She was happy for Raoul, but there's no way she wanted to continue their communication.

"Jakeshia, it is my honor to award you the title of Valedictorian for the nursing class of spring 2007!" As Jakeshia walked up to the stage, confetti was thrown and the graduation song began to play. She was so happy and nervous at the same time. Not only was she a first-generation college graduate, she was graduating with honors. Her family was so proud of her accomplishments. She had stayed focused while going to school, worked, lived independent of her parents, and had broken generational curses. That day marked the beginning of her true legacy.

"Thank you, Dr. Jones and the entire nursing program faculty. It is truly my honor to stand before everyone today and accept this medal along with my diploma. The past two years have been extremely challenging yet rewarding." Jakeshia continued on to give her speech for about two minutes. She talked about the neighborhood she grew up in and her daily environment. She spoke about the good and bad experiences she endured throughout her twenty-two years on Earth. She even mentioned her constant dedication to making her mom proud to show that all of her hard work did not go in vain.

"Emory class of 2007, I want to leave you all with a few words of encouragement as you take this next leap into your future. Sometimes you must reinvent yourself, start from scratch, unlearn everything you thought you knew, and even break yourself down. Do not be discouraged when things don't appear to be in your favor. Life has a way of putting us in uncomfortable spaces. Be patient, keep your faith, don't fold, and continue putting your best foot forward. You have everything you need within you to prevail and be successful. I thank you for your time. It has truly been an honor to speak before you today, and again, I wish you the best of luck on all your future endeavors!" Jakeshia's speech was followed by an abundance of clapping from the crowd. The ceremony continued as she sat on the stage for another hour. Once the ceremony ended, she met up with her family and friends, who welcomed her with hugs and kisses. She was extremely happy but exhausted. Her mom was throwing her a graduation party the next day, but Michael had plans to take her to a celebratory dinner when they left the Georgia World Congress Center.

Jakeshia arrived at her mom's house to see most of her immediate family, non-immediate family, Michael's family, and her friends. The music was blasting as everyone congratulated her as she entered. "Oh my god!!! When did this happen?!" She was shocked to see Jamaal standing next to his pregnant girlfriend, Denise.

"Hey Jakeshia, girl. I'm four months pregnant, and we'll find out the gender next week." She hadn't seen her friends in months since school had her super busy.

"Well, congratulations to you two! I am so happy for y'all." Jakeshia gave the two a hug and continued to circulate the party. Her mom set everything up in the backyard. There were five tents, a bunch of food, alcoholic and non-alcoholic beverages, cake, cupcakes, and a snow cone machine. Her younger cousins were running around playing tag and throwing a football. Her aunties and older cousins were sitting down discussing senator Barack Obama, who was running to be the first African American president of the United States. Michael came up behind her to give her the biggest hug. They parted ways the night before since he was helping her stepdad and mom cook the food.

"Hey, my valedictorian nurse!" Michael handed her a dozen roses.

"Hey, my handsome engineer." They smiled at each other intensely.

"Get a room, why don't ya!" Marissa said annoyingly as she walked over to give her little sister a hug. "Baby sis, I'm so proud of you! I taught you everything you know, now look at you!" They both laughed. Jakeshia really did run behind her sister growing up. She used to dress like Marissa and even borrowed her clothes to do so.

"Thank you, big sis. If it wasn't for me watching you and learning from you, I wouldn't be here today." The two talked a little bit before Jakeshia went to go fix a plate of food. She sat her plate at the table with Michael's family, because they looked out of place. They knew how to have good, innocent fun, but Michael's family was not accustomed to big gatherings.

"Hey familllly, I'm so happy you could make it!" She made her way around the table to hug everyone.

"Baby, you are our daughter too. We wouldn't miss this. You have made us all proud." Olivia got teary eyed. In the short amount of time that Jakeshia knew Michael's family, they had truly embraced her. There was no difference between them and her family. She knew she was locked in with them for life.

"Keshia, come up here and open your graduation gifts." Her mom called her to a table that was full of envelopes and a box. She walked over to the table and began to open up the envelopes, which were all full of money and gift cards. As she opened each, she was calculating the total in her head. By the time she finished, she had a total of $3,000.

"Wow, you all are so generous! I really appreciate each and every one of you for coming to my celebration. This journey was very challenging, but with everyone's motivation and support I am officially a registered nurse! I haven't told many people, but I will be starting my new career next month working for Emory University Hospital!" Jakeshia paused while her family clapped and gave their words of praise. "I will be working in the emergency room, which is where I finished my clinical experiences." While she continued to talk and give various thank you's, Michael walked around fixing a glass of champagne for all the adults. Once he finished, he walked over to Jakeshia, took the microphone from her, and handed her a glass with her name on it.

"Alright everyone, I just want to do a toast for my intelligent, beautiful, hard-working fiancée. Raise your glasses and let's toast to her completing four intense years of college. Let's toast to her new career as a nurse. Finally, let's toast to her taking the necessary time to care for herself as much as she cares for others. This one's for you Jakeshia. Cheers!" Michael clinked glasses with Jakeshia before everyone chugged their champagne. "Now that my beautiful fiancée has a little time to herself, I want to present her with my graduation gift." Michael handed Jakeshia an envelope. She opened the envelope and got teary eyed. There were two round trip tickets to Aruba. She had never been on a plane before, so she was excited that her first trip would be to Aruba. She had heard many great things about the warm ocean water and the gentle breeze of the wind. She was overwhelmed and could no longer talk. The only thing she could utter was, "Thank you."

Everyone spent the remainder of the party talking, dancing, and laughing. As Jakeshia looked around, she was thankful. This was what karma looked like when you sowed good and positive seeds. She knew in her heart that karma worked in her favor. Before she and Michael left her graduation party to pack for their trip, her spirit told her to speak one last time. "Family and friends, again I want to thank you for coming here to celebrate with me. I am full and content as I look around at each of you. I want to challenge you to take the next thirty days to be intentionally positive and intentionally happy. At times, I find that we focus so much time and energy on negative factors, opposed to looking at the bigger picture. We are responsible for the path and the distance we travel in life. Every season is meant for your success, so stay focused." She smiled as she left her mom's home. She was genuinely at peace and anxious to enjoy paradise.